# Starting Over

*For Mum,*

*with love, always!*

*Jen*

## Jen Silver

Affinity
eBook Press
NZ
2014

Starting Over
© 2014 by Jen Silver

Affinity E-Book Press NZ LTD
Canterbury, New Zealand

1<sup>st</sup> Edition

ISBN: 978-1-927282-96-0

Editor: Ruth Stanley
Cover Design: Irish Dragon Designs

# Acknowledgments

I would like to thank, first of all, Affinity E-book Press for taking a chance on publishing my work. Also many thanks to my beta readers and my editor, Ruth Stanley, for their encouragement and good advice.

Thank you also to Nancy K for a wonderful cover design.

Thank you to my mother who has always supported me in my life choices, however daft they may have been.

Most of all, thanks to my partner, Anne, who puts up with me daydreaming my way through life, and gives me the space, the time and above all the love, to achieve my dreams.

# Dedication

For Anne, with love

# Table of Contents

*Starting Over*

Part One

# Chapter One

## Introductions

Robin carried her coffee out to the old stable block, the single-story stone building across the farmyard. It was their studio and already she could hear the pottery wheel turning. Ellie was concentrating on the clay in her hands, throwing another pot. Robin didn't disturb her, going straight to her own work area. There was a pattern forming in her mind, a swirl of colour she wanted to experiment with. Her coffee cooled as she tested different combinations on her artists' sketchpad. The colours had looked brighter on the screen of her laptop but fine adjustments with the paints were needed to make the pattern come alive as it had in her imagination.

"Looks good, Rob." Ellie had come in quietly and was leaning against the doorframe, her hands still covered in wet clay.

Putting her paintbrush down, Robin went over to her and lightly brushed the loose strands of blonde hair away from her face. "So do you."

Ellie sidestepped her before she could move in for a kiss. "Don't. I'm not in the mood."

"No, I guess not." Robin stood still, looking down at the earthen floor.

"Why is she coming here?"

"She asked."

"You could've said no. We had an agreement..."

"I know. But, well, things have moved on a bit. She wants to see where I live. And, she wants to meet you."

"Why? So we can compare notes?" Ellie paused. Looking up, Robin could see plainly the pain in her normally clear blue eyes. "Like what a shithead you are," she added before turning and stalking out.

Robin leant back against the rough stone wall and closed her eyes. It had obviously been a mistake. Ellie wasn't ready to meet her lover, maybe she never would be. But she hadn't been able to say no to Jas when she asked to spend her week off with her, here.

Here was the pottery business she and Ellie had built up over the last nineteen years at Starling Hill, an isolated former sheep farm perched amongst the rolling hills above the town of Huddersfield in West Yorkshire. At first they had barely covered costs, selling pottery at market stalls and arts and crafts fairs. Their overheads were low because the farmhouse and land belonged to Ellie's family. But with the advent of the website boom in the late 1990s they had gradually built up a solid customer base. Ellie had initially stuck to making standard stoneware items, establishing a range of distinctive mugs, plates and bowls, all with a trademark starling imprint. With the website set up to take online orders at the turn of the century, she started making bespoke tableware sets. Recently, she'd expanded her repertoire to create raku-style vases, using Robin's design skills to produce a recognisable Starling Hill style.

When Robin first met her, Ellie was living at the farm with her mother and teaching at the local secondary school. Her subject was history but she also taught a few geography and geology classes. One of her favourite parts of the school year had been accompanying a group of keen sixth formers on a yearly geology residential field trip to Arran. Ellie's interest in archaeology, and Roman history in particular, had led her to want to try making her own pottery. It amused her to think that in a thousand years remnants of her pots would be found and an expert would enthuse to a multiverse-wide

3

audience, "Oh, yes, definitely one of the Eleanor Winters range, 1990 AD or thereabouts." She had learned to throw pots at an evening class and continued to develop her skill by setting up a work area in the stables with the help of another local potter and her mentor, Kieran Taylor. The farm, by then, consisted only of a dozen laying hens and two goats. When the goats died the old stable, a long, low-ceilinged building, was converted into a workshop with her pottery wheel and kiln. The stalls had been knocked together and partitioned off from the main pottery area. This was where Robin mixed paints and experimented with different styles for the glazes.

Taking a deep breath, Robin thought about the last time she had been with Jas, her London lover. On her most recent visit to the city, she had met her from the train and they'd gone straight to a restaurant for dinner. By mutual consent they decided to skip the dessert course and barely made it back to Jas's flat with all their clothes on. Lovemaking with Jas wasn't often a gentle business, and she'd been particularly intense that evening. Robin could still feel the scratches on her back where Jas had raked her long nails. Even though she enjoyed the sessions with Jas, there was nothing she would have liked more right now than to be able to crawl into bed with Ellie and hold her close.

Maybe it was age catching up with her, she would be forty-three on her next birthday. She had only been twenty-four when she met Ellie, having previously had no thoughts whatsoever of settling down with anyone. In her line of work at the time she could sleep with a different woman every night. Falling in love hadn't been part of her life plan. Falling in love with a woman ten years older with a teenage son was something she would have laughed at had anyone suggested it could happen. It wouldn't happen to her.

Starling Hill farm had been her home, as well as her main place of work, for the last eighteen years—apart from the hiatus when Ellie had her midlife crisis the previous year. They still hadn't fully recovered from that, but after several months of pain and indecision they had decided they could manage to live and work together. Sometimes Robin thought it was like a married couple staying together for the sake of the kids. In their case, the kids were the pots.

✝

Ellie sat at the farmhouse kitchen table, her hand wrapped protectively around a mug of coffee. She usually enjoyed the peace of working in the early predawn hours before Robin stirred. And, usually, she could handle Robin's presence, absorbing herself in her work. But she'd hardly slept since Robin told her Jas was coming to stay for a week. She had lost more than one night's sleep in the last few months as she realised this woman, whom she'd thought was only one more of Robin's flings, had gained a foothold in Robin's affections. The knowledge that it was her fault didn't help her gain any peace of mind.

If only she hadn't given in to what she thought now had been a mad impulse to sleep with someone else. Sleep with— one of the English language's most misleading euphemisms—it had been lust, pure and simple. And at the time it had been exciting and helped assuage her feelings of desperation at reaching fifty. Somehow fifty seemed too old. Too old for someone like Robin. Their ten-year age difference had bothered her right from the start. She had kept Robin at arm's length for several months after their first meeting, but Robin kept coming back. And Ellie wouldn't entertain the idea of them living together while her mother was still alive. Her mother thought Robin was a boy—*so polite and helpful, that boy. When's he coming back, Ellie?*— she would ask after each one of Robin's visits to the farm.

Robin had played up to her shamelessly, always calling her Mrs Winters. Nothing was too much trouble; she would fetch and carry whatever her mother wanted. Ellie smiled at the memory of the three of them together watching television, her mother in her chair with everything she needed within reach; Robin seemingly absorbed in whatever was showing on the screen, but in reality using the hand that was out of range of her mother's limited vision to caress her breasts.

It hadn't been a romantic way to meet. Ellie had been travelling back to Huddersfield after another fruitless meeting with her ex-husband about Aiden's upbringing. She had little enough say in it as it was, only seeing her son every other weekend. Having just made the decision to leave her teaching job in order to look after her mother, she had asked Gerry if Aiden could spend more of his upcoming summer holiday at the farm. Gerry had been his usual uncompromising and condescending self, reminding her why she didn't have custody and wasn't fit to be a mother. The fact that Ellie's affair with the woman she had left him for was well and truly over, didn't make any impression on him.

The midweek, midafternoon train from Manchester wasn't full and she had been pleased to get a seat at a table, plenty of space to wallow in her misery. The train had left the station and was starting to pick up speed when she became aware of someone plonking down in the seat opposite, someone who thoughtlessly dumped their bag in front of her and scrabbled through it, throwing items on the table. It was only when the stranger finished rummaging and reached up to put the bag on the overhead shelf that she realised it was a woman, getting a close-up glimpse of her bare midriff as she stretched.

Her annoyance reached a crescendo when this female yob then settled down in the seat, put headphones on and turned up the volume on her Walkman so loud that Ellie could recognise the tune.

"Excuse me," she said loudly. No response. She snapped her fingers in front of the girl's face. "Turn it down!"

"What?"

"Turn it down, or go and sit somewhere else."

The stranger paused the music and looked at her. Ellie was immediately struck by the intensity of the young woman's hazel-brown eyes. "What's your problem?"

"The problem is the train's half empty and I would like to sit here on my own without having to listen to your crappy taste in music."

Shrugging, the stranger said, "Sure. No problem." To Ellie's surprise she calmly took the headphones off and wrapped the cord around the Walkman, then put it down on the table between them. "Do you mind if I just sit here and look at you instead?"

"What...?"

"Sorry, that was a bit rude. My name's Robin." She grinned at her.

"Why would you want to sit and look at me?"

"You looked so sad."

"Do you think my mood's improved having you invade my space?"

"Maybe not. But if you want to talk about it, I'm a good listener."

And strange as it seemed to her afterward, Ellie opened up to this stranger. She told her about the meeting with her ex-husband, her worries about her son, her mother's fragile state of mind, her new lack of career. And Robin told her nothing about herself. Only when she mentioned that she was setting up a pottery studio in the stables did Robin say she would like to see it. Before Ellie knew it she'd invited her to visit the farm.

†

Jasmine would be arriving in a few hours. Unable to concentrate after Ellie had walked off, Robin wandered out to the chicken run. The hens ignored her as usual and carried on clucking about, searching for things to eat on the barren ground. Ellie had names for them but she couldn't tell them apart. They were, she knew, all named after Roman goddesses. The only ones she could remember were Minerva, Venus, and Luna. The roosters were called Jupiter and Apollo—she suspected they were gay, as they seemed to spend their days in each other's company, cowering on the other side of the compound from the hens.

The total absorption of the fowl in their search for food was soothing to watch and calmed her nerves. She should never have agreed to let Jas come to the farm. Ellie was right—they had an agreement. When she returned, after Ellie said the affair with Kathryn was over, they had both said it was to be on a strictly professional basis. If either of them wanted to have affairs, that was fine, just don't bring them home. And so far, she'd stuck to it. But the liaison with Jas had lasted longer than most, maybe because they only met up every few months when she visited London to meet with clients.

Her part of the pottery business didn't occupy her full time. She made more money with the sideline of creating websites; it had been a natural progression from her original career as a graphic designer. When she met Ellie, she'd enjoyed a productive and exciting few years designing CD covers for some of the top bands in the UK and Europe. She had been travelling back from a gig in Liverpool when she met Ellie on the train. Well, met wasn't exactly the right word for it. She'd spotted her from the platform before boarding the train and been immediately enchanted. Maybe it was just the aftereffect of five testosterone-filled days and nights in the company of an all-male group, but she wanted to reach across the table to this woman and kiss away the sadness from her face.

Leaving the hens to their constant pecking, Robin walked across the yard and leant against the fence. She never tired of the view, across the meadow and beyond, the wooded hillside on the other side of the valley. It was a magical place. She'd felt it on her first visit when she'd ruined the tranquility of the scene by roaring up the farm track on her motorbike. Ellie had greeted her coolly, introducing her to her mother and playing hostess with a spread of tea and scones. When Mrs Winters finally fell asleep in her chair, Robin urged Ellie to show her the pottery setup. She had been impressed with the work even though Ellie said she was still at the experimental stage.

It was starting to get dark when Robin managed to steal a first kiss. Up to that point she still hadn't been sure she was on the right track with Ellie, just trusting to instinct that she was one of her persuasion. The kiss hadn't been entirely satisfactory. Ellie pushed her away.

"I don't think this is a good idea," she said.

"Why not? Feels good to me."

"Do you ever think before you do anything?"

"No. It just complicates things. Ellie, I want you. What else is there to think about?"

"Maybe about whether I want you."

"I think you do."

They were standing a foot apart and Robin could no longer see her features clearly. But she could feel the pounding of her own heart. Ellie made no move towards her. Finally she turned away and walked slowly back to her bike. She didn't know whether to laugh or cry as she rode off, laying some rubber with a bitter sense of satisfaction.

The next few weeks had been busy with a new commission. And although she found some solace with one of the group's castoff groupies, a sixteen-year-old sexual tourist, thoughts of Ellie kept intruding at inconvenient moments. When the final proofs had been signed off, she couldn't block out her feelings anymore and found herself somehow riding in the hills above Huddersfield on a mission; this time she wouldn't be dismissed so easily.

Partway up the long climb to the farm, she saw a hitchhiker. Brushing aside considerations of moors murderers, she pulled in ahead of the forlorn-looking figure. She realised, with relief, that he was only a young lad, fourteen at the most. "Hey, where you headed?" she asked, not removing her helmet.

"Starling Hill farm."

"Bit of a trek, then." It was still three miles, at least, and that was just to the end of the mile-long track leading to the farm itself.

"Yeah, missed the last bus. My mum's going to kill me."

"Hop on, then, and hold tight." She smiled to herself. This must be Aiden.

"You sure? Wow! Cool." He climbed on behind her eagerly.

She took it slowly, making sure he was safe, but he seemed at ease leaning into the curves. When they arrived at the farm, he hopped off nimbly. She set the stand and climbed off, removing her helmet.

"Gee, thanks, that was great. I hope I haven't taken you out of your way."

"Not at all. I was on my way here. Aiden, I presume. I'm Robin."

He shook her outstretched hand, "No shit. I mean, my gran thinks you're a boy. She keeps asking Mum—when's that nice boy, Robin, coming again?"

"Yeah, I know." She winked at him. "Maybe best not to tell her otherwise."

Ellie had thanked her politely for giving Aiden a lift, but not before she'd given him an earful about the perils of hitchhiking. He disappeared into the house, leaving Robin standing awkwardly again, feeling about fourteen herself. Ellie had that effect on her.

"So," she said, arms folded protectively across her chest, "you just happened to be passing?"

"Yeah. Seemed like a nice evening for a drive out in the country."

"Robin, I can't..."

"Ellie, please." Robin found the courage then to move and place herself in front of Ellie. She placed her hands gently on her shoulders. "Please, just let me hold you."

Their first real kiss. Robin had never forgotten it. All her senses were on fire and she was certain Ellie was feeling the same way with the heat radiating from her body and the soft yielding of her lips. But then she had pushed her away again saying she couldn't do this with her mother and son in the house. Robin wasn't used to being rejected but she somehow knew that if she persevered it would be more than worth the effort. Ellie wasn't just another meaningless conquest. She was a formidable challenge and gaining her trust was the driving force for Robin. When Ellie did finally let her in, the passion she ignited was something Robin had never encountered with any other woman.

Now, so many years later, she was experiencing that frustration all over again. She was sure that on some level Ellie wanted her but Robin knew she was going to have to work a lot harder now to gain her trust once more. Too much history, too many lapses, the latest of these now on the way to the farm. Robin didn't know how she was going to get through this day let alone a week. Ellie was right. She should have said no.

✝

11

The second time around the ring road and Jasmine felt she'd entered one of Dante's circles of hell. Hadn't she passed the university twice now? She had trusted Robin's directions rather than the sat-nav, which Robin told her was useless in this area, likely to direct her to the bottom of a reservoir, a drowned village from the past, like Atlantis.

Then she saw it, the exit she wanted, but she was in the wrong lane and there was a constant flow of traffic either side of her. She was doomed to make another pass of this circle. The circle of the damned! What had she done to deserve this version of hell?

Falling in love with Robin. Could that be counted as a heinous sin? It had started as a casual one-night stand, and then expanded to a series of one-nighters, sometimes two, whenever Rob visited London. Now she was hooked; she wanted more. And what was she going to find at Starling Hill farm? Whenever she tried to fish for more information, Robin would deflect her. So far she'd only learned she lived there with her business partner. Googling it, she scoured the pottery business website for clues. There had only been one small photo of the potter, Eleanor Winters; a black and white professionally shot publicity photo, which didn't give any useful information like hair or eye colour. Even so, the woman didn't look like someone who would attract Robin. Rather mousy, she thought. But she obviously had some kind of hold over her lover.

What was it that Robin wouldn't tell her? Well, she was going to find out for herself, if she ever got off the Huddersfield ring road.

Arriving at the farm an hour later than planned, Jasmine was in a foul mood when she finally drove into the yard. Negotiating the narrow lanes hadn't improved her state of mind; fear of another car coming around each uphill twist and turn or having to brake suddenly for sheep crossing had her worrying for the silver metallic paintwork on her precious C Class Mercedes saloon. It was a company car but she prided herself on keeping it in prime condition.

There were several vehicles parked up, an ancient Jeep, an equally ancient Corsa, and a much newer, sleek black Harley Davidson motorcycle. At least the presence of the bike showed that Robin was here. She pulled into the space next to the rust-heap of a car and climbed out, feeling the stiffness in her knees. Her lower back screamed at her as well. Damn! She should have taken the train.

The place looked deserted, in spite of the number of vehicles. The house had a lonely, forbidding air, its narrow windows and grey stone façade giving it a decidedly gothic look. She gazed at the other structures: a chicken enclosure and a run-down barn. Trying the house first seemed the best option. Knocking on the door, she wondered again if this hadn't been a colossal mistake. A quick cup of tea and she would head back to London.

The door opened when she pushed on it. Of course. She was in the country now. Feeling like an overdressed burglar she stepped into the gloom of a low-ceilinged room.

"Hello!" Only the ticking of a clock from somewhere in the room greeted her entrance. "Anyone home?" Christ, how could anyone want to live here? The deathly quiet atmosphere was starting to creep her out.

She reached into her bag and pulled out her phone. No messages. So, Robin hadn't even been concerned that she was late. Angrily, she clicked on Robin's name in her Contacts list. She hadn't driven two hundred miles to be ignored. Into the silence came the sound of Robin's ringtone. She followed the sound into the kitchen. The ringing stopped as she reached the device, sitting on the counter next to a mug of cold coffee. A large ginger cat on the window ledge opened one eye and closed it again.

"Fuck's sake, Robin! Where the hell are you?"

"And, who, may I ask, are you?"

Jasmine turned around and found herself looking at the mouse-like creature from the website. Older than she had expected, the photo on the website must be twenty years old, at least, but blonde, blue-eyed and unfortunately, more attractive than the picture suggested. She put on her best smile and held out her hand. "Jasmine Pepper. You must be Eleanor."

The woman ignored the proffered hand and walked past her. She filled the kettle and put it on the Aga, which Jasmine now noticed took up one wall of the kitchen. Without turning from the stove, the other woman said, "Robin's in the studio."

Sensing that was all she was going to get in the way of conversation, Jasmine said, "Okay. Thanks." She found her way back out into the yard. The studio must be in the dilapidated-looking barn thing. For the second, or possibly third, time that day, she thought she should cut her losses and head back to civilisation.

✝

Robin had given up trying to work. She played another round of *Temple Run 2*. Her stats on the endless running game weren't great but she enjoyed watching Scarlett's butt swinging across the chasm on a rope. The intrepid explorer escaped from the Temple with a stolen treasure and outran the demonic ape, collecting coins and powerups, until disaster struck and she fell off a cliff. Robin knew her concentration levels were at low ebb if she couldn't travel fifteen hundred metres on the game without meeting disaster. *RUN AGAIN? Sure, why not?* Robin tapped the button on the screen to restart the game. Ellie had pushed her away, again. Not without cause, but she wasn't sure how long she could bear it. She had come back to the farm because she wanted to be near Ellie. The separation had been hard and she wished they could both turn back the clock and start again. The sound of the outer door of the stables opening distracted her and Scarlett crashed headfirst into a tree. Putting the iPad down, she went through to the pottery studio hoping it was Ellie. Instead she came face-to-face with Jas, standing in the middle of the room looking extremely pissed off.

"Hi," said Robin from the studio doorway.

"Thanks for the welcome. Are you even bothered that I'm here?"

"Yes, I am...bothered, that is."

"Well, great. I'll just sod off back to London, shall I? I'm looking forward to spending another hour on that fucking ring road."

"Look, Jas, it was your idea..."

"You didn't say no, did you?"

Robin shrugged.

"So, do you want me to stay, or don't you?"

It shouldn't be like this, thought Robin. But it would never have happened if Ellie hadn't taken up with that other woman. The biter bit, she couldn't handle the thought of Ellie with someone else but Ellie had put up with her fucking any woman who crossed her path when she was on the road. And now she was treating Ellie the same way Gerry had, unable to forgive one single mistake.

And here was Jas. A one-night stand that had gone on too long, demanding more from her than she could give. "Do you want a drink?" she asked, moving past her towards the outer door.

"You know what I want, Robin." Jas followed her outside into the startling brightness of the afternoon sunlight.

"Is Ellie inside?"

"Yes."

"Okay. Wait here." Robin set off towards the house at a run.

Ellie was in the kitchen, sitting at the table, Soames sat contentedly on her lap enjoying the sensation of her fingers stroking him; long, leisurely strokes, starting at the top of his large ginger head continuing down his spine and caressing the length of his tail. Both Ellie and the cat had their eyes closed, but only Soames was purring.

Robin watched from the doorway. *Lucky Soames.* It had been a long time since Ellie had stroked her with such tenderness. It seemed a shame to disturb them but she needed to move forward to get to the fridge. She had just reached out to open the door when Ellie opened her eyes.

"What do you want, Robin?"

"A couple of beers."

"That's not what I meant."

"I know." Robin took two beers from the fridge then turned to look at Ellie. She had closed her eyes again. Soames, though, had jumped off her lap at the sound of the fridge door opening and was now curling around Robin's legs, looking up at her hopefully. *Fickle beast.*

The silence between them lengthened. Robin could feel the cold bottles warming in her grasp. Even Soames gave up on her and stalked off somewhere. *What did she want?* The question she had been avoiding since coming back to the farm, now out in the open.

*I want you,* was the answer waiting to be spoken. And now, just as she was on the verge of saying the words aloud, Jas appeared at her side. She slid a possessive arm around Robin's waist and asked, "Are you going to open those, babe, before I die of thirst?"

Robin looked over Jas's head and saw Ellie's mouth quirk into a smile. She could almost see the speech bubble erupting...*Babe!* She'd never live it down. And Jas had her pinned to the counter so she couldn't move unless she shoved her unceremoniously away.

Ellie stood up, found the bottle opener and passed it to Jasmine on her way out of the kitchen. "There you go. Enjoy, babe!"

Jas helped herself to one of the bottles Robin was holding and popped the cap. Freed from her grasp, Robin moved away from her. She picked up her phone, lying where she'd left it. Clicking it on, she saw she had three messages, all from Jas.

"I guess she doesn't like me. I thought you said it was finished between you two. Looks like unfinished business to me."

Robin didn't say anything. She opened the Facebook app on her phone.

"So, yeah, I get it now. You have this cosy little setup here and then just play away. It works, as long as you keep things separate."

Robin kept her eyes on her phone. Status updates and a message from Aiden. Stopping by for a visit on their way back from Glastonbury...he and Sophie had some news for them. Probably getting married. They'd been together for a few years now and Aiden wasn't getting any younger, he'd been thirty-three on his last birthday. That was okay, she liked Sophie and marriage would be good for Aiden.

"For fuck's sake, Robin. Do you think you could even look at me? You've said hardly a dozen words to me since I arrived."

"Glastonbury. That was this weekend, wasn't it?"

"Shit, I don't know. I'm not interested in that hippie crap. Robin, are we going to talk about this?"

"Sure. But not right now. I've got to do some shopping."

"What?"

"Supplies. Ellie's son is on his way to visit and he still has the appetite of a horse."

Robin started for the door, grabbing keys from the dish by the door.

"Fine. I'll come with you."

†

"How do you think they'll take the news?" asked Sophie as they continued their journey up the M6. Having spent two nights in an overpriced yurt at the festival, they'd stopped over in Marlborough to visit friends on Sunday and were now on their way up north. Seeing the Rolling Stones in concert had been the highlight of the Glastonbury weekend, and Aiden was still on a high.

"They'll be cool."

Sophie smiled. Although Aiden was six years older than her he often sounded six years younger, at least.

"I expect Robin will be cool but I'm not sure about your mother."

"She'll be good. It's just the kind of boost she needs. She's had a rough year."

"I wish they'd sort it out."

"They will."

They lapsed into silence. Sophie knew that Aiden's connection with Robin was in some ways stronger than with his mother. He'd had years of conditioning from his father, telling him his mother didn't want him, that Ellie had abandoned him when he needed her most. And although they'd built a fragile bridge over his teenage years, it was mainly through Robin. As an adult he was able to see that his mother wasn't the evil witch his father had made her out to be, but it was hard to shut out the swirling emotions he'd felt as a five-year-old.

She slept for the rest of the journey, only jerking awake as Aiden turned off the road onto the track leading up to the farm. Sophie sat up and looked around. She loved Starling Hill, especially at this time of year when the sunlight on the hills brought everything into sharp focus. The bare hillsides, sheep grazing in the distance, clouds moving slowly across the clear blue sky, marred only by the occasional fading jet trail. The views of the wooded hills across the valley moved her as well. She put a hand on Aiden's knee. He turned his head to smile at her; she knew he felt it too.

He turned off the engine and looked around the yard. "Mum's out, I guess, the Jeep's not here. We should've phoned."

"I'm sure she won't have gone far."

And sure enough, at that moment, the Jeep came roaring up the lane behind them and juddered to a stop not far away. Robin leapt out and slammed the door. She looked extremely hot and bothered with her hair was sticking up, her shirt hanging out of her jeans. Sophie wanted to laugh; there were times when Robin reminded her of Heathcliff. She had that kind of wild, sexual energy associated with Haworth's most famous fictional son.

Her smile froze, though, when she saw the woman who had climbed out of the passenger seat and come round to meet Robin at the back of the Jeep. Robin yanked the back door open and pulled out a bag of groceries. She shoved these at the woman and said something to her. The woman gave her what could only be described as a lecherous grin and swaggered off into the house.

"Isn't that...?" Sophie whispered.

Aiden looked as shocked as she felt. "Yes." He opened his door and got out. "Hey, Rob, need a hand?"

Robin smiled when she saw them. "Great timing, guys. You can carry the beer, Aid."

"What's she doing here?" he asked, somewhat aggressively, Sophie thought.

"Who?"

"You know who! We watched her go into the house just now...Jasmine bloody Pepper."

"How do you know her?"

19

"Had to work with her a few times."

"Sounds like it wasn't a great experience."

"She's a prize bitch. So, what's she doing here, Rob?"

Robin closed her eyes and leant against the side of the Jeep. "Look, could you just take the beer? I'll bring the rest."

Sophie jumped in then, sensing Aiden wanted to continue probing. "Come on, love. I'm dying for a pee."

Aiden picked up the box and set off towards the house. When Sophie looked back, Robin was still leaning against the back of the vehicle with her eyes closed.

"What's that all about?" Aiden still sounded peeved.

"It's not too hard to figure out."

Aiden staggered, almost dropping his load. "No way! Robin wouldn't bring her shit here."

"Doesn't look like she had much choice. Doesn't look like she's too happy about it either."

†

Ellie reached out to touch the paint palette Robin had been working on earlier. She could see what she was trying to achieve, another Japanese-style design. If only she could talk to her. For weeks she'd been working herself up to talking about this stupid agreement. Then Robin dropped the bombshell about Jasmine and she was back to square one. She went through a range of emotions each day—pent-up desire for her ex-lover, anger, and self-recrimination. Unable to contain the feelings Robin's touch in the stables had ignited any longer, she gave in to the tears that had been threatening since their early morning encounter.

Just as she was giving in to a good old cry, a ball of fur landed in her lap. Fleur, mother of Soames, looked up at her with bright green eyes. The comfort of cats, Ellie thought, as she started to stroke her.

There was a time when they would talk, or rather, she would talk and Robin would listen. She was, as she'd said at their first encounter, a good listener. One day, not long after the evening she had rejected Robin's second clumsy advance, they had bumped into each other in the town centre. She had been trying to find a birthday present for Aiden, searching through the rock section at HMV, at a loss, when a voice at her shoulder said, "No, I don't think so," and there was Robin, grinning at her. "Something for Aiden, you won't find it here." She steered her over to another section and quickly picked out the latest CD of a well-known rap artist.

"I can't give him that. I'm his mother."

"Yeah, and he'll think you're really cool."

She not only let Robin persuade her to buy the CD but to have coffee with her. Ellie found herself telling her things she wouldn't have said to anyone, even her mother.

She told her about the guilt she felt, about her affair that had cost her the right to bring up her child. She hadn't been sorry about the breakup of her marriage; meeting Susan had opened her eyes to a depth of relationship she'd never experienced before. And being in love, truly in love, for the first time in her life, she had been blind to the effect it had on her husband. And he had used that to ensure he was granted custody. It hadn't gone to court because she was afraid to fight it, afraid she would lose her job as well if they had a public battle.

Robin bought her a large cappuccino and a blueberry muffin and listened. After a time she reached over the table and put her hands over Ellie's. "Look, in a few years, he'll be able to choose. And, I think he'll choose you."

"Why? Why would he choose me? All I've ever done is abandon him."

"At some point he'll realise how much his father manipulated the situation. You're not a bad person. Why wouldn't he love you?"

Jen Silver

Ellie found herself looking into Robin's eyes and was caught by the intensity, like a rabbit frozen in a car's headlights.

"I want to love you, Ellie. Won't you give me the chance?"

And, from that moment, Ellie was ensnared. She invited Robin to come for tea that evening. After her mother had gone to bed, they made love for the first time, on the living room floor. Robin's passion had overwhelmed her; she seemed to instinctively know all her erogenous zones, unerringly inflaming every nerve in her body. Luckily her mother was a sound sleeper as well as being hard of hearing. Ellie hadn't thought she was capable of making noises like the ones Robin's hands, tongue, and writhing hips, brought forth from her.

And when her mother died in the spring of 1995, having succumbed to a bout of pneumonia, she was happy for Robin to move in with her. Robin had already started helping her develop the pottery business with sales and designs.

She had never expected Robin to stick around, this twenty-four-year-old who acted closer in age to her son. When Aiden was there it was like having two teenage boys— they were messy, left clothes wherever they shed them, jam jars open on the countertops, noisy music blared from the radio—talking endlessly about groups she'd never heard of. Unknown to her at the time, Robin took Aiden to his first music festival when he was fifteen. It was one of the weekends when he wasn't with her so she couldn't even be angry with her. If anything had gone wrong, Gerry would have been blamed as the careless parent. She knew she had Robin to thank for the thawing in her relations with her son, but it was Robin he adored. Ellie was under no illusion about that, she was clearly only tolerated by association.

During her time with Kathryn, Aiden had only visited the farm once to pick up something he'd left in his room.

Even though he was over thirty, she'd kept his room for him in her attempt to remind him he had a home with her. As soon as Robin returned he was back to visiting on a regular basis. She knew they communicated these days via Facebook and Twitter. She only had an email account because Robin had set it up, insisting she needed to join the twenty-first century and go digital. But she couldn't get to grips with it.

And now it had come to this. She desperately wanted to talk to Robin again but there was a barrier between them. At first, it was the barrier called Kathryn. She knew how hurt Robin had been and she couldn't even explain to herself how it had happened. Then when it was over, Robin had reacted much the same way as Gerry over her earlier affair. So, the business with Jasmine, when it started, was no doubt just another way to punish her.

"Mum! Are you in here?"

Ellie started and Fleur jumped out of her arms. She hadn't been expecting a visit from her son.

"In here," she called, standing up and brushing herself down. She wiped at her face, hoping it wouldn't look too blotchy.

Aiden came in and, unusual for him, pulled her in close and hugged her. "What's happening, Mum? Why is that woman here?"

Ellie started to shake. She let him hold her close as she calmed herself, steadying her breathing. Aiden wasn't much taller than her; they weren't a tall family. At five foot five inches, he hadn't grown much since he was fourteen, but he felt solid, good muscle tone.

"She loves you, Mum," he whispered in her ear.

"Funny way of showing it," she mumbled into his shoulder.

"I don't think Rob's that pleased to see her. It's obviously a mistake."

*Jen Silver*

"A mistake!" Ellie pulled back from him. "One of many. Why am I the only one around here not allowed to make mistakes?"

She ran out into the yard, her eyes blurred with tears. And stopped. Was it a mirage? Coming slowly up the track from the road, a colourfully painted VW van, looking as if it had emerged from the mists of time, 1968 at least. As it drew closer, she could see the driver, a woman with long curling hair, and next to her a dog, paws on dashboard looking eagerly around.

†

Robin shot out of the farmhouse front door. The day was taking on the surrealism of an art house movie. The camper van came to an abrupt shuddering stop in the middle of the yard. She could see Jo's wide smile through the windscreen before she opened the door and her large black-and-white dog streaked out and jumped up to lick Robin's face. Jo followed, more sedately.

"Harry, leave her alone!" Jo pulled the dog off and made him sit.

"Jo! What are you doing here?"

"You invited me, don't you remember?" She moved in for a kiss as well.

Robin held her off, aware now of Ellie standing near the stable door. "Um, not really."

"Sure, you said to drop in if I was ever passing. And here we are." She beamed, opening her arms wide, expecting Robin to welcome her more warmly.

"Well, I..." Robin was at a loss for words.

Ellie came over and bent down to stroke the dog. Then she straightened up and said to Jo, "Hi, I'm Ellie. Welcome to Starling Hill. Would you like a drink...tea, coffee, something stronger?"

24

Jo looked from Robin to Ellie and back, then she smiled at Ellie. "Yes, a cup of tea would be great. Do you mind if Harry comes in as well? It's too hot to leave him in the van."

"Oh, I'm sure he'd like a look around the farm. He seems to know Robin." She turned to look at her business partner. "Just don't let him bother the hens." Ellie took Jo by the arm and led her towards the house, leaving Robin gaping after them.

The night spent in Jo's van was one Robin remembered well enough, the mingled smells of incense, dog, and sex. That she'd invited her to visit the farm was lost in the ether.

Aiden came out of the stables in time to see his mother walking into the house with a strange woman and Robin standing and looking down at a black-and-white dog that was looking up at her expectantly. He walked around the camper van and came to stand next to her. "Who's that, Rob? One of Mum's arty friends?"

"No."

"Then, who...fuck's sake, Rob. Not another one?"

Robin shook her head, slowly. "Come on, Harry," she said to the dog and started to walk towards the field.

Aiden followed. "Rob, what's going on here?"

"I don't know. I wasn't expecting her."

"But you were expecting the Pepper woman?"

"Yes."

"So, who's she?"

"Just someone I met in Hebden Bridge a few months ago. She let me use part of her stall at the market to sell pots."

"So you slept with her? As payment?"

Robin shrugged. "Yeah, well, we don't make much profit."

"Oh, I guess that makes it okay then."

"Look, I'd totally forgotten about her until I saw the van just now."

"Is that where you did it? In the van?"

"Oh, grow up, Aiden. Since when did you care who I sleep with or where?"

"Since you're hell-bent on hurting my mother by bringing your casual fucks here."

"She didn't care much when she took up with what's-her-name."

"Jesus, Robin. That was one woman to how many in eighteen years? Like she said to me just now, why is she the only one not allowed to make mistakes around here?"

Robin stopped and looked at him. "She said that?"

"Yeah. And if you ask me you're just as bad as my dad? You wouldn't believe the things he used to say about her. It's taken years to shake off the brainwashing he inflicted on me. I grew up thinking she was a wicked scarlet woman only concerned with her own gratification. Seems to me now that her only crime was falling in love with the wrong people."

"Does that include me?"

"Yes."

"She knew what she was getting into when we met."

"I somehow doubt that. Look around you, Rob. This is her life. She's a country girl..."

"She's not stupid, if you're trying to make out she's some kind of country bumpkin."

Harry raced joyously around the field, stopping to lift his leg and sniff at everything in a high state of excitement. Robin leaned against the fence with Aiden stopping a few feet away from her. She could feel the tension radiating from him.

"You're like him, you know?" he said finally.

"Like who?"

"Harry. Running around, marking out your territory. They'll run out of blue plaques...Robin Fanshawe slept here with...fill in the name..."

"Very funny."

"And, you're not getting any younger. Middle age for women starts now—mid-forties—you're already over the hill."

"Gee, thanks. Glad you didn't take up social work."

"Just saying..."

"I hate it when people say that!"

"So, what are you going to do about these two?"

Robin turned her head to look at him. He was still in an aggressive stance, looking like he wanted to punch her. "Jo's not a problem. She's more interested in the pottery. I remember now, I did say she should come and have a look at the setup." She looked back over the field. "Jas will leave if she doesn't get what she wants."

"And will she get what she wants?"

With a deep sigh, Robin turned back to look at him again. "No. It's over. She just doesn't know it, yet?"

"What do you want, Robin?"

"We both know the answer to that. But does she want me back?"

"Oh, I think so. But you two need to talk."

Robin picked at the wood railing and called Harry. The dog bounded over and wriggled through the gap, his whole body shaking with joy. Robin reached down and rubbed his ears. "Where do I start, Aiden? I've really screwed up this time, haven't I?"

"How about telling her you love her."

"Oh yes, she's really going to believe that with Jas trying to rip my clothes off every time I'm near her."

†

Inside the house, Ellie sat in the kitchen and listened to Jo talk. She was something of a free spirit, she realised, with a touch of envy. Jo managed to make a living creating knickknacks out of a wide variety of materials, mostly scraps

27

and things other people discarded. Dream catchers were particularly popular, she told Ellie. Fusing plastic bags to make wallets and belts, this had gone down very well when Hebden Bridge had declared itself a plastic bag free zone. She had even made Harry a dog bed from old towels. When Robin had pitched up at the market to sell some of Ellie's pottery, she had been inspired, she said. She had always wanted to learn how to make pots.

Ellie was aware of Jasmine sitting at the opposite end of the kitchen table, nearest the door, stifling a yawn. She was sucking on another beer bottle. Pathetic, thought Ellie, a woman her age trying to look like someone younger. At least Robin could pull it off with her youthful, boyish looks and the way she acted. This woman was trying too hard to be hip, or whatever the term was now. Stylishly cut shoulder-length black hair, possibly her natural colour, framed a rather square face. The plucked eyebrows really didn't do her any favours. Maybe it was the in thing in the big city. What Ellie knew about fashion of any sort wouldn't have filled the blank side of a postage stamp.

As far as she knew, Sophie was lying down in the cool of the living room, listening to her iPod. No doubt trying to stay out of this, whatever this was. A trio of Robin's women sitting in the kitchen, all very different. As she'd always suspected, Robin wasn't fussy about who she shagged; only needing a willing body. At least Jo had an attractive personality, and possibly a good figure, although it was hard to tell with the loose, flowing garments she was wearing. She recalled the sign on the Burnley Road coming out of the town with the wording, *That was* so *Hebden Bridge*. These people are so up themselves is what she'd thought at the time. Now, she thought, maybe the wording on the sign was representative of the cultural time warp that was Hebden Bridge. Everything about Jo screamed 1968, flower power, free love, make peace not war...from the brightly painted VW van to the flower print skirt and Birkenstock sandals, to the not-so-subtle whiff of patchouli oil, no doubt masking the smell of an illicit substance...the hills are alive with the growth of marijuana plants.

Watching Jasmine out of the corner of her eye, idly peeling off the label on the beer bottle, Ellie realised that neither of these women could possibly threaten her way of life. She liked Jo and thought that perhaps it really had been a one off with her and Robin. Jasmine, though, was something else. She wanted Robin and nothing was going to stand in her way. Ellie could almost see the wheels of her mind turning, plotting to lure Robin away to the big city. If she thought that was going to happen, she was deluding herself. She obviously didn't know Rob that well.

†

Jasmine yawned again. It was warm in the kitchen and, as far as she was concerned, these two women were certifiable. Nothing they said made any sense to her. How could you make money out of recycled rubbish? Well, maybe you could if you were prepared to live in a shit-hole like this. It was possible, she thought. God knows what it was like in winter. The barren landscape had few redeeming features, even now at the height of summer.

Robin couldn't possibly want to stay here. She could offer her so much more. Jas had been in no doubt of what she wanted on the long drive up from London. There were other women in her life; women who helped fill the lonely nights when Robin wasn't there. And although she had known these women longer than she had known Robin, spent more time in their company—going out to plays, conversing at dinner parties—it was Robin who set her pulse racing. Whenever she knew Robin would be in the city she cancelled any other plans. They spent most of their all-too-brief times together in bed, or out of it—the living room floor, the shower, the kitchen counter—Robin had fucked her in just about every position, everywhere in her flat. It made her smile for days afterwards whenever she remembered where Robin had last touched her, last caressed her breasts, licked her from top to bottom, literally.

And now, here she was—a stranger in a strange land—with no reference points, unaware of the local rules. Robin drew away when she touched her. She had tried to reach out to her while they were driving back from the supermarket. Jas was desperate for some acknowledgment from her lover, any sign at all that she wanted her.

But Robin brushed her off at every turn. It surely couldn't be the mouse-woman. They didn't act like they were lovers. And checking out the upstairs rooms when she went up to use the bathroom, it looked like they slept in separate bedrooms. As for the hippy-dippy woman, someone Robin had met at a market, a market for weirdos it sounded like listening to Jo's stories, no worries there. She just needed to get Robin on her own. It shouldn't be beyond her.

Sophie appeared in the doorway then. With her tousled, sleepy look, the younger woman immediately drew the attention of the three older women in the kitchen. Jas remembered now where she'd seen her before. It was at a high profile company's fiftieth year celebration when she'd had a stand-up row with the boss of the events management company. Sophie had been there in the background with her boyfriend, Ellie's son. She'd clocked the good-looking blonde, but hadn't really taken much notice of the man she was with, even though he'd waded into the argument as well, obviously a minion of the arsehole she was reaming out.

"Are we going to eat anytime soon, Ellie?" Sophie asked. "I'm starved. We didn't stop anywhere on the way up from Marlborough."

Looking at her youthfully rounded limbs and full-looking breasts, Jas didn't think there was any danger of the young woman wasting away through the lack of one meal. However, Ellie immediately got up. "Of course, sweetheart. Let's see what Rob managed to forage from the supermarket." She didn't look at Jas when she added, "I'm sure Aiden or Robin will show you around the pottery studio."

Jo, of course, offered to help prepare the meal, but Ellie shooed her out. And Jasmine followed, if only to see if she could indeed get Robin on her own.

# Chapter Two

## Complications

Kathryn Moss sat in her book-lined study staring at the computer screen. It had seemed a simple thing when lying awake at two in the morning. After all there hadn't been any acrimonious split—they had just drifted apart. First a week passed, then two, and before she knew it six months had gone by. She'd had a busy time, working on a new research project as well as tutoring her PhD students. Sometimes, with her students, she felt more like a social worker than a professor in archaeology. But it was no excuse for not staying in touch. And she knew Ellie would be interested in her proposal, the chance to get her hands in the dirt again and do some real fieldwork. It certainly excited her, although Kathryn knew her role would be mostly supervisory, monitoring her students as they gained valuable field experience. All she had to do was pick up the phone—Ellie didn't do emails—and most of the time didn't answer the phone either.

After a fruitless hour of fiddling with things in her office, tidying the shelves, drinking two cups of coffee, Kathryn decided a phone call wouldn't do. She had to see her face-to-face.

Retrieving her newly purchased sporty red Honda Civic from the car park, she headed out of town, and wondered why she hadn't done this before. Meeting Ellie and spending time with her at Starling Hill had been a welcome diversion during the winter and early spring terms from the mundane routine of teaching and marking papers. Their affair had been brief but very sweet. Towards the end, she had sensed that Ellie's heart wasn't really in it. She knew there was someone who had shared her life for a long time, but who was now absent for some reason.

It was a lovely summer's evening and she enjoyed the drive, but she couldn't help feeling more and more anxious as she turned up the track to the farm wondering what kind of reception she would get from Ellie after the months of silence.

The number of vehicles in the yard was an unwelcome surprise. It looked like she had visitors. Kathryn almost turned the car around, but curiosity won out. She parked next to the VW camper van that looked like a mirage from the 1960s. Knowing Ellie never locked her front door, she knocked lightly, and then entered the house. The smell of cooking hit her right away—vegetarian lasagne, possibly. Opening the door to the kitchen she found herself being scrutinised by six pairs of human eyes and then jumped on by a black-and-white border collie.

"Harry, no!" The woman nearest the door grabbed at the dog's collar and stopped him from licking Kathryn's face.

"Hi," Kathryn said gamely. "Hope this isn't a bad time."

"Not at all." Ellie got up from her place by the Aga and walked around the table. "Would you like some lasagne? There's plenty to go round."

"Yes, thanks."

"Okay. Rob, could you fetch the chair from your room?"

"I'll get it." The only male, apart from the dog, jumped up to do her bidding.

"Thanks, Aiden. Introductions, then. This is Kathryn Moss, well, actually, Doctor Professor, or is it Professor Doctor?"

"Kathryn will do." She smiled.

"Right. This is Jo," Ellie continued, indicating the woman holding the dog. *Judging by the way she was dressed,*

33

*the owner of the van,* Kathryn thought. "Robin, who also lives here, sometimes." *Ah, the errant lover.* "Sophie, my son's girlfriend." *The youngest person in the room and likely a few months pregnant, from the glow of her skin.* "And Jasmine, who drove up from London today to see Robin." *Good grief, what had she walked into?* The young man returned then with the extra chair. "And this is my son, Aiden."

Sophie had, meanwhile, produced a plate and cutlery for her and Jo moved over so she could sit down between her and Robin.

"What would you like to drink, Kathryn? Wine, beer, water?" This from Robin, establishing her credentials as joint head of the household.

"A glass of red wine would be great, thanks."

Aiden pushed a glass towards her and Robin stood up to pour from the bottle on the table. So, this was the competition. A bit more butch than she'd expected. Robin had the lean boyish good looks that she knew some women favoured. Perhaps not for much longer if she guessed her age right, bordering on mid-forties. The short reddish brown hair and green eyes gave away her heritage. Some Irish blood there, but then most natives of the British Isles could lay claim to Irish ancestors.

"So, Kathryn," said Robin as she regained her seat at the table, "what do you profess?"

"Archaeology."

"Oh. Guess that explains it."

Kathryn had just taken a mouthful of lasagne so all she could do was raise her eyebrows in response. But the message was clear enough.

"Wow, that's amazing," enthused Jo, the dog owner on her right. "Do you get to do any digs, like on *Time Team*?"

"Usually during the summer break. In fact, we might have one coming up." Kathryn looked at Ellie as she said this, hoping to signal a subliminal message across the table, but Ellie was looking down at her plate and poking at the food as if it held the answer to one of the great mysteries of the universe. She would have to get her on her own. The enormity of what she would be asking hit her again and the professor took a big gulp of wine. She was aware that everyone at the table, to varying degrees of interest, was checking her out. Not unlike tutoring a group of post-graduates, only perhaps with more hostility than curiosity emanating from some of those around the table.

Kathryn recalled the first time she'd seen Ellie. She hadn't felt much like going to the evening lecture, but Ed was her best mate in the faculty, so she'd gone to give him moral support. He'd been worried that only a handful of the super nerdy undergraduates would turn up, more out of duty than a desire to listen to him drone on for two hours about forensic archaeology. She had assured him that he didn't drone and they would be turning people away at the door.

Ellie stood out as being older than the other members of the audience, clearly not a student but dressed like one wearing a faded baggy Oasis T-shirt and worn blue jeans, moccasins on her feet, as if she'd left the house without putting her shoes on. Captured by the blonde hair framing a heart-shaped face and intense blue eyes, Kathryn had approached her as she stood looking pensively at the brown liquid that purported to be coffee.

Talking to her had been easy. Kathryn didn't make a habit of picking up women but there was something about Ellie that immediately attracted her. Her relationships seldom lasted more than six months. Finding someone of equal intellect with an attractive personality had so far eluded her and time wasn't on her side, having reached the downhill slope of fifty-two. It was a revelation to meet someone who wasn't obsessed with modern gadgets. One of the things she noticed on her first visit to the farm was the lack of televisions in either kitchen or bedroom, and no widescreen monster in the living room. The downside was trying to reach Ellie without the modern channels of 24/7 communications. She didn't text or email, wasn't on Facebook or Twitter. Her mobile, which was just a phone, was usually switched off or out of juice. And there was no phone in the pottery studio. It was only when she noticed the switched off Wi-Fi router in a corner of the living room that she found out about Robin.

In terms of intellect, Ellie ticked all the boxes. They talked about common interests—Roman history, books, and archaeology. She also had a lovely smile and, when Kathryn finally saw her without a baggy T-shirt and loose-fitting jeans, an extremely attractive body. So, why had she let this one drift away? Obsessed with her research projects, conferences, and lecturing commitments, as usual.

Sitting in the dean's office a few days earlier, this had all seemed straightforward. Now she wasn't so sure. How could she have even imagined Ellie would welcome any disruption to her quiet, well-ordered life? Not so well ordered now it seemed, Kathryn thought, looking around the table at the disparate group gathered there.

Taking another large gulp of the wine, which was surprisingly good, she turned to Jo. "And what do you do?" It would be useful to know how the dog owner fit in with this menagerie. When she visited the farm she had been surprised Ellie didn't have any dogs. Living on this remote hilltop, she would have thought a dog essential, not only for company, but also for a sense of security. Ellie confessed to being a bit dog phobic. True to lesbian stereotype, she preferred cats.

Jo beamed at her. "I'm a craft-worker, and I met Robin at a market when she was selling some of Ellie's pottery. I told her I was interested in seeing how a potter worked and she invited me to come and have a look, so here I am."

"What kind of things do you make?" Kathryn asked, more out of politeness than a desire to know.

"I recycle..."

"Rubbish," muttered the one who'd been introduced as Jasmine, and who stood out as being overdressed for a visit to a farm.

"Well, one person's rubbish could be another person's treasure," Jo said equably.

"Oh, you mean like wind chimes made from compact discs. I've seen a lot of those recently." This came from the girl, Sophie.

"Yes," said Jo enthusiastically. "They're very popular."

"Certifiable." Another barely audible comment came from the obviously disaffected Jasmine.

"I'll put the coffee on," Robin said loudly.

"Yes, I'm afraid we haven't got dessert." Ellie started clearing plates.

"Oh, I forgot. We brought some chocolates. God, I hope they haven't melted, they're still in the car." Sophie started to get up.

"I'll get them, love. They should be okay." Aiden disappeared.

†

What did Kathryn want? It had been months since they'd stopped seeing each other. Well, whatever the reason, the timing couldn't be better. Robin's face had been a picture when she appeared. No doubt she'd been imagining her as a frumpy bluestocking intellectual. Instead she was faced with the reality of an attractive brunette, going grey at the sides, but that and the half-moon glasses only added to the air of authority. She wasn't as tall as Robin, but she commanded attention with her confidence and charm.

Robin and Aiden had taken charge of making coffee, finding cups or mugs for everyone, spoons, sugar, and milk. Ellie sat in her living room watching the way the other women arranged themselves. Kathryn had pulled up the desk chair to sit near her. Sophie sat on one end of the sofa and Jo politely seated herself on the other end, leaving a space in the middle for Aiden. Jasmine perched on the stone shelf by the fireplace. The animals had found their own spaces. Harry was curled up on the floor in front of Sophie. Soames and Fleur were keeping their distance from the dog; Soames watching everything from the top of the bookcase under the window, Fleur stretched out on the back of Ellie's chair, pretending to be asleep. Robin hovered about for a few minutes, finally bringing in a chair from the kitchen and sitting as far away as possible from Jasmine.

Ellie knew at some point this evening she would have to talk to Kathryn on her own. But for the moment she was enjoying seeing Robin's discomfort at the situation. Sleeping arrangements would be interesting. What if Kathryn wanted to stay the night? She found she wasn't averse to this idea but in reality she knew Kathryn had another agenda.

She relaxed into the chair, its thick arms enfolded her and she felt calmness descend. This chair was a part of the family. Her father would sink into its depths after a hard day of working on the farm; then it had become her mother's refuge during her last days, everything she needed placed within reach. As a child, if either parent or cats didn't occupy the chair, Ellie would make it her own space. She retreated into the chair on those long, lonely evenings when Robin wasn't there. She didn't want to dwell on where her erstwhile lover was on those nights, no doubt in the arms of another woman.

It was one of those evenings, a Friday night in November, when she'd decided to go to the lecture she'd seen advertised in the paper. It was time, she thought, to explore some of her interests. Archaeology had once been a burning enthusiasm. She'd participated in summer digs during her university days. Recalling those long hours, scraping through layers of soil, sometimes unearthing an object that qualified as a genuine find, it seemed to Ellie that was when she'd been happiest.

Talking to Kathryn about her work during their long walks had brought it all back, a journey through time to her twenty-year-old self. She didn't want to dwell on the present. Reaching the age of fifty had been painful and she hadn't felt able to discuss her fears with Robin. Soon she would be the same age her mother had been when she died, having already passed the landmark of her father's early death at the age of fifty-one.

The lecture took her out of herself for a few hours and when Kathryn spoke to her afterwards she had found herself opening up to this stranger in much the same way she had when she first met Robin on the train.

Kathryn was trying to catch her eye, but Ellie focused instead on the unusual sight of Robin setting out coffee cups and playing host. Now that she'd had time to think about it, there could be only one reason Kathryn had called in person. Weeks earlier, when she'd spotted the low-flying aircraft circling overheard she'd been expecting to hear from her ex-lover. It wasn't far, in terms of miles, the distance between her house and Kathryn's, but it had taken on the span of a light-year or two in the silence of the intervening months.

She knew that Kathryn didn't think she had noticed the time she'd spent pacing around in the field. Or the time she'd left their bed early to dig some holes in the ground, stooping to examine something closely. When she'd returned to the bedroom after that secret foray, Ellie had pretended to be asleep. That morning had been the last time they made love and she'd sensed impatience in Kathryn's movements.

After she left, Ellie went into the field to see where she'd been digging. It didn't look like anything had been disturbed; well, she was an experienced field archaeologist. What had she found? Ellie decided she wasn't going to ask.

†

Robin surveyed Kathryn carefully. So this was the mystery woman who had found a way past Ellie's reserve, for a short time anyway. She didn't think she could possibly still be a threat. Ellie had gotten it out of her system. She wasn't a natural philanderer. But there were looks passing between them, looks she couldn't decipher. Kathryn was here for a reason. This doctor professor, whatever, wouldn't have turned up out of the blue without an agenda. She would be trying to get Ellie on her own. Well, that wasn't going to happen, anymore than she was letting Jas corner her again.

The only one here without any hidden motive seemed to be Jo. She was genuinely interested in the pottery studio. Robin thought Ellie should just put her on to Kieran. He was, after all, her mentor in the pottery business. They shared the running of evening classes through the winter months and Kieran used their kiln to fire his own creations. But he was, she recalled, in Australia visiting his son and newborn grandchild.

Jo seemed to be quite taken with Kathryn and was addressing her again, "...always loved *Time Team*, especially the guy with the colourful knitted jumpers. And that bloke from English Heritage—he made me laugh. He'd wander off for most of the programme, leaving everyone else scraping away like buggery in water-filled trenches, then turn up hours later with a big smile on his face like he'd just been to Narnia and met the faun."

Kathryn just smiled at her enigmatically. Shit, why couldn't Ellie have fallen for someone less attractive and obviously successful? Sneaking looks at Ellie, she could see she wasn't upset to have her ex-lover here, if she was an ex. It balanced things up a bit. All she needed now was for the long departed Susan to turn up, and maybe Gerry for good measure.

"Oh, I just love the Narnia books," piped up Sophie. Robin had thought she was asleep in her corner.

Kathryn smiled at her—*did she ever stop smiling?*— Robin thought, uncharitably. However the professor's next words stunned everyone in the room. "That's great. I'm sure you'll enjoy reading them to your child. When are you due?"

Sophie opened her mouth then closed it again, looking to Aiden for help.

Aiden looked at his mother apologetically, "Sorry, Mum, we hadn't expected you to have so much company. We were going to tell you when we got here."

Watching the conflicting emotions move across Ellie's face, Robin wanted to go to her and hold her close. She was going to be a grandmother. Hitting fifty had been huge, and now this.

Jo was the first to break the silence. "Oh, that's fantastic news." She patted Aiden's arm. "This calls for a celebration." She stood up and rushed out the front door.

Ellie moved then and went over to hug both Sophie and Aiden. Robin met Aiden's eyes over his mother's shoulder. She smiled at him. So this was what they had come to tell them. And the fact they had made the journey in person instead of plastering the news over their Facebook page meant a lot—something she would have to explain to Ellie later.

Jo bustled back in carrying a guitar. Even having spent just the one night with the woman, Robin knew her repertoire consisted mainly of sixties folk songs and felt sure they were in for a rendition of "Blowin' in the Wind," but if she started with "House of the Rising Sun" she'd be finding herself out the door before reaching the first verse.

As Jo started strumming, Robin caught Sophie's words to Ellie. "Yes, it's a girl. We've had a scan."

"Have you thought of a name?"

"Bit early for that, isn't it?" muttered Jasmine, looking more and more like the bad fairy not invited to the feast.

"Well, our first choice is Wren," said Aiden.

Ellie looked at him questioningly. "Wren?"

"We wanted the name of a bird, but not Robin, obviously."

Robin stared into the empty fireplace. This wasn't going to help thaw relations with Ellie. She would have expected at least her mother's name or her middle one to be first choice. But then Jane and Freya weren't likely candidates for a modern young couple naming their first child. They should just be thankful the baby wasn't going to be saddled with Chardonnay or Chlamydia.

Jo was humming softly to herself. Then Kathryn piped up. "Wren's nice, but there are other more popular bird names these days...Raven, Ava which is Latin for bird, or even Merle, which is blackbird in Latin."

*Show-off,* thought Robin, adding out loud, "Or there's Jay...handily androgynous if she turns out to be on our bus."

"How about Thrush?" offered Jasmine. They all turned to look at her. "Well, it's a bird. Or there's Blue Tit, that might go down well in these parts."

"Shut the fuck up," said Robin, giving Jas a hard stare.

True to form Jo started singing a folk song, one that Robin recognised from Ellie's ancient record collection, a Julie Felix song, "We Wish You Love." The soothing rhythm and gentle words wafted into the room. She had to give Jo her due; she wasn't as flaky as she looked. Signalling to Aiden with her eyes she went into the kitchen.

"Congratulations," she said when he followed her in and closed the door. "I'm sorry if this visit hasn't gone to plan for you. I guess it's my fault."

"Well, Kathryn turning up hasn't helped."

"She wasn't to know."

"No." Aiden came over and gave her a hug.

"What's that for?"

"I don't know. I just think I'm going to need some help with this. Parenting, I mean."

"Yeah, well, it's not something I have any experience of."

"Still, I need you...to be around."

Robin held on to the counter for support. "Aiden, I'll always be there for you. Whatever happens with me and your mum."

"You don't think she's really interested in the professor woman, do you?"

"I don't know. She's not what I expected. I mean, I can see the attraction for your mother. She's more intellectually suited."

"Not much fun if all you want is a good fuck."

"Jesus, Aiden. You're going to be a father. And is that all you think I am to Ellie?"

"You think the walls here are soundproof?" He gave her a penetrating stare, his unblinking blue eyes disconcertingly similar to his mother's.

"Oh great. Hope we didn't warp your little mind during your impressionable teenage years."

Whatever Aiden planned to say didn't come out of his mouth as Ellie came through the door. She gave Aiden a hug and whispered something in his ear. He nodded, grimaced at Robin and left.

"So, do we call you Gran or Nana?"

"If you say either of those words to me again, I'll bury you headfirst in the chicken run." Ellie burst into tears.

Robin moved in for a hug and let Ellie cry on her shoulder. It felt good to hold her even though it wasn't likely to lead to a release of the sexual tension Robin had felt building all day. With Ellie's heaving breasts moving against her, it was all she could do to hold back from slipping her hands under the sobbing woman's shirt. The softness of her hair and closeness of her body was intoxicating.

Ellie finally gathered herself and pulled away. "I'm sorry. It's just been a bit much, today of all days."

"I'm sorry, too." Robin took a deep breath. There was so much she wanted to say. But the right words wouldn't come. "Look, I don't think Jas will stay long. She'll probably leave tomorrow."

Ellie didn't seem to have heard. "I don't want to be a grandmother. I'm pleased for them, of course. But...oh God, Robin...why do we have to grow old?"

"Happens to all of us. But, hey, let's help them celebrate tonight. Jo, at least, has the right idea." Robin took seven glasses out of the cupboard, an assorted collection of wineglasses and tumblers. She fished around in the drinks cabinet until she found the dusty bottle of Remy, that usually only saw the light of day at Christmas, and an unopened bottle of Jameson's whiskey. "Not having any champagne on ice, this will have to do." She placed all the items on a tray then looked over at Ellie. "Any idea why Professor Doctor whats-it has dropped in?"

Ellie wiped at her tears with the back of her hand. "Oh yes. I have a very good idea." She looked up at Robin then. "And it's not what you think."

†

The house was still at last. Kathryn had gone home; Jo and Harry were in the camper van. Jas was on the pullout bed in the study that only occasionally served as a guest room. Robin had given up her squatter's rights to Aiden's bedroom so the young couple could sleep there and had bedded down in the living room. Ellie knew without looking at the bedside clock that it was around two a.m.; there was that middle-of-the-night stillness she recognised. Groping for the glass of water she always kept by the bed she found only empty space. Of course, with all the shuffling round, finding sheets and towels for people, and most of all, Kathryn's request before driving off, her routine had been shaken and she'd forgotten to bring a glass up with her.

Opening her bedroom door quietly she crept down the stairs to the kitchen. Coming out with her glass she peeked into the living room. Robin was sprawled across the sofa, wearing only a pair of boxer shorts. She'd left the lamp on; the whiskey bottle nearby looked mostly empty. Ellie stood transfixed, watching Robin's bare chest rise and fall, her small breasts offering a tantalising vision. She wanted to curl up next to her and wake up in the morning with Robin's arms around her and her mouth on her lips, and then her hands moving down her body. Taking a deep breath she moved stealthily across the room and switched the lamp off. Robin stirred but didn't wake. Ellie returned to her room and lay awake staring into the dark.

She wanted Robin's touch. Sex with Robin was always an adventure. She aroused a violent passion in her that she hadn't known she possessed. Susan, her first female lover, had been gentle and reassuring in bed, probably because she knew she was Ellie's first; long slow sessions of kissing, fondling, exploration of each other's bodies with hands and then tongues. It had been undemanding, comforting. With Robin it was an entirely different matter. She would sometimes tease Ellie by taking her time, but more often than not, she would dive straight in. Kathryn's approach was somewhere between the two.

Meeting at the coffee urn after the lecture, Ellie had been attracted by Kathryn's ready smile and easy manner, not professor-like at all. She was also the same height and it was, she decided, very nice to be able to look directly into someone's eyes without having to look up all the time. Several coffee dates later, and a stroll along the canal, came an invitation to dinner. Kathryn's house was everything Ellie would have loved if she hadn't inherited the farm. Book-lined walls, matching furniture, and the house was in Lindley, one of her favourite parts of the town. After a lovely vegetarian meal—Robin ate whatever she put in front of her, and then disappeared to fill up on meat products—and a bottle of wine, Kathryn had asked tentatively if she would like to stay the night. And she had, without hesitation, said yes.

It seemed unreal to her now, how easily she had capitulated. Kathryn was only the third woman she had ever slept with. It had been good for a time and then it just sort of fizzled out. Kathryn stopped calling and Ellie realised, eventually, that she wasn't interested enough to find out why.

Now, this sudden reappearance. With the arrival of first the unpalatable Jasmine—what on earth could Robin have been thinking? But then, Robin didn't think—and then the rather sweet but scatty, Jo—the sight of Kathryn hadn't been too much of a shock. When Kathryn did finally manage to find her on her own, coming into the kitchen just after Robin left with the tray of glasses and brandy, she came straight to the point about what she wanted.

Yes, she had found something in the field that last time she visited the farm. She'd sent the samples away for testing and had her intuition confirmed—definitely second century Roman. This had prompted her to fund the aerial survey herself. She had the photos in her car if Ellie wanted to see them. There was a clear outline of a settlement and given the height of the farm, it could have been the site of a useful observation post.

"Ellie," Kathryn had exclaimed the night before, betraying an excitement Ellie hadn't seen in her before, "this could be the biggest find in this area—since the discovery of Melandra Castle near Glossop—and that was fifty years ago! If I'm not mistaken, I would guess that some of the stone used for your stables, and possibly the foundations of this house, would have come from the original buildings out there. But apart from that there's little chance of much other disturbance from treasure trove hunters up here. The dean's agreed to funding a dig; we'll be able to use student volunteers, ideal for them to gain fieldwork experience locally."

"How long would it take?"

"It's not a large area, but to do it properly, I would say eight to ten weeks. But we would have to start soon. It's already late in the year—ideally we should have started in April, giving us a good six months."

"You mean you can't do it in three days."

"That's a made-for-TV fantasy. It doesn't happen like that in the real world. And this will be a real coup for the university."

Ellie agreed to think about it and let her know by the weekend. Kathryn had pressed her to try and make a decision before that but then backed off when she saw the look on Ellie's face, a closing down she recognised all too well.

Kathryn had left the photos with her before she drove away.

How could she not agree? This was one of her dreams come true, a real live archaeological find, here, on her property. Kathryn had assured her that the university would pay for any damage and would backfill and returf the field once the dig was finished. Although if English Heritage got involved they might want it preserved as a site of historical interest. In which case, she would have to consider selling the field.

Ellie was sure there would be a lot more to the excavation than just Kathryn and a handful of keen archaeological students turning up with trowels and buckets. They would need a digger to remove large sections of sod and create trenches. Would they bring their own food or have a catering van on site? Portaloos were also likely needed. She wasn't having them traipse through the house to use the facilities.

It was the middle of the night and she couldn't possibly sleep with this going around in her mind. Dressing quietly, she crept out of the house and across the yard to the pottery studio. Humming to herself she set about getting some clay ready, preparing it to go on the wheel. She had offered to show Jo the process.

Also nagging at her consciousness was the baby, due in December. She didn't doubt that Sophie had the maturity to handle motherhood; she wasn't so sure of her son's ability to adapt to being a father. But he had a good job and they had recently bought a house. Sophie said she planned to keep working until the end of November. The solicitors she worked for had promised to keep her job open for her to return to after her maternity leave.

And it wasn't just the thought of being a grandmother. Gerry would be the child's grandfather and she wondered how much influence he would try to exert. Before they'd gone to bed, Aiden had taken her aside and told her they were going to ask Robin to be a godparent and hoped she didn't mind. She told him it was okay with her, but she thought to herself that Gerry wouldn't be happy about it. He couldn't stand Robin and wouldn't want her corrupting his grandchild.

She had asked Aiden if he and Sophie would be getting married. He just shook his head and said, "One step at a time, Mum." She wondered if he had given it any thought at all. What surname would they give the child? Hopefully they weren't going to hyphenate Greenwood-Caffrey. On the other hand Wren Winters wasn't a bad option.

Ellie shook herself. None of these thoughts were leading anywhere. Time to get the coffee on; she needed to be properly awake for the day ahead.

# Chapter Three

## Decisions

Robin stirred, aware of the cold. She had been warm when she fell asleep; the effects of too much brandy and whiskey mixed. Not normally a heavy drinker she felt nauseous when she tried to stand. Pulling her T-shirt over her head she struggled to get her arms into the armholes.

The smell of coffee pulled at her nostrils. Struggling into her hastily cast-off jeans, she stumbled into the kitchen.

"Oh good, you're awake. I didn't want to disturb you." Jo greeted her brightly from the other side of the room by the Aga. "I've made coffee. Would you like some?"

Robin nodded, accepting the cup gratefully. She took a sip and was surprised to find it was a good strength. Jo had only offered her tepid fruit tea when she'd stayed the night with her. "Is anyone else up?" she managed to croak out after swallowing the first mouthful.

"Ellie's in the pottery studio. I thought I'd take her a cup. How does she take it?"

"Milk, no sugar. Where's Harry?"

"In the van. I wasn't sure about letting him roam about on his own."

"I'll take him out to the field. Could use some fresh air."

"Yeah, you look a bit rough."

"Thanks."

"Robin, you don't mind me being here, do you? I hadn't realised you and Ellie were...you know."

"Were...that's right. We're just business partners now."

"And, Jasmine...she's..."

"History."

"Oh. I wasn't sure. And what about Kathryn? Pretty cool, huh. A professor in archaeology. How did Ellie meet her?"

"I don't know. You'll have to ask Ellie. Look, thanks for the coffee. I'll go to the loo and then I'll take Harry for a walk, okay?"

"Yeah, thanks. I'll take the coffee over for Ellie. She's going to show me how to do it...make a pot, I mean."

"Great." Robin found that standing up was an effort. She made it to the downstairs toilet in time to throw up. Never again, she thought. It was never a good idea mixing drinks. Totting up her intake of the day before she realised she'd had beer, wine, brandy, and whiskey. And she hadn't eaten much. Slowly cleaning up after herself, she went back into the kitchen and drank some water, then headed out to Jo's van to collect Harry.

The dog was thrilled to see her, and after jumping up to lick her face he bounded off in the direction of the field. Robin followed more sedately, trying not to open her eyes too far; the sun was just coming up and casting a golden glow over the yard. She would have preferred a bit of gloom to match the pounding in her head.

Had coming back been such a good idea? She really had thought she could handle it. But seeing Ellie on a daily basis just brought back the hurt. And it hurt mostly because she knew it was her fault. Ellie had put up with her scratting around like a teenager in heat, yet she couldn't cope with the idea of Ellie with someone else. And seeing that someone in the attractive shape of Doctor Professor Kathryn Moss had hit her hard. Although, she couldn't deny Ellie deserved better than she'd ever given her.

There were a few design jobs in the pipeline. Maybe it was time to make the break properly. Find a bolthole. She couldn't crash at Aiden's now that he and Sophie were properly nesting. And Rick had made it clear—after their bust-up at the attempt to have a family Christmas had back-fired—that he wasn't keen to see her anytime in the near future. She seemed to have a talent for causing chaos wherever she went. But was it really her fault if Rick's girlfriend had responded to her approaches so willingly? Was it her fault if her brother was a failed rock star and couldn't handle his now deadbeat nine-to-five lifestyle?

She called to Harry who had found something interesting at the far end of the field. He ignored her and carried on digging frantically. Walking carefully over the uneven ground, Robin went to see what he was obsessed with. It was something brown, long and thin. Processing it gradually through the haze of her hangover, Robin came to the realisation that it was a bone and probably not an animal one.

"Shit, Harry. Leave it now. Come on. Harry!" She pulled at his collar, he growled at her.

Deciding that neither he nor the bone was likely to be going anywhere, she turned and ran back up the field.

†

Ellie had just taken the clay out to show Jo the final stages of preparation before setting it on the wheel when Robin ran in. She looked wild, but Ellie was used to seeing her with her hair standing up on end, clothing in disarray, usually as a result, though, of frantic foreplay.

"Jo! Come quickly. Harry's found something, he won't leave it."

Jo looked at her blankly. "What?"

"He just growled at me."

"What is it? What's he found?" Ellie wiped her hands on a towel. Jo had already left the studio.

"You might want to call Professor whats-it."

"Kathryn. Why?"

"It's a bone."

"So?" Ellie still didn't feel properly awake. "It could be an animal's."

"Looked a bit too big for any animals around here."

"You don't mean..."

"Yes."

"Shouldn't we call the police then?"

They were walking quickly towards the field. Robin pulled out her phone and handed it to Ellie. "Go on. Phone her. She'll know what to do."

"It's a bit early."

"She didn't look like a person who lolls about in bed...unless there's someone in it," Robin couldn't resist adding.

Ellie grabbed the phone and punched in Kathryn's number. She moved away from Robin to listen to the ring tone, hoping Kathryn had already left for work. To her relief the answering service came on asking her to leave a message. "Uh, hi Kathryn. I was..."

"Ellie!" Kathryn's voice broke in on the recording.

"Hi, look, I hope I didn't wake you."

"Not at all. But I didn't expect to hear from you until later in the day, or possibly the week."

"I...well, it's not about that. Could you come up to the farm today?"

"Why, what's up?"

"Jo's dog...he's found a bone in the field. It may be human. We're not sure what to do."

"Has he dug it up? Can you try and make sure it's left in situ? I'll be up as soon as I can. I may bring a colleague...he's a forensic anthropologist specialising in osteology. Well, you know him, Ed McLaughlin. You came to his lecture last year. See you soon. And don't worry."

Ellie handed the phone back to Robin. "She's coming." Glancing down the field she could see Jo struggling with Harry. "We'd better go and help Jo." They set off together.

"So, what's the other thing?"

"What other thing?"

"You said you weren't calling her about that?"

"She wants to do a dig here. She's found evidence of a Roman settlement."

"Really? You mean this bone could be a Roman soldier's?"

"Well, that would probably be a better option than the remains of a local serial killer's victim."

"So, are you going to let her dig?"

"I wasn't sure last night but I think this find sort of makes it inevitable. It'll happen now whether I want it to or not." Ellie was struggling to keep her emotions under control. Robin reached out and Ellie let herself be pulled into an embrace. Feeling Robin's enfolding arms, her lean frame pressed up against her, all the pent-up tension of the last week poured out and she sobbed freely.

"Ellie, I want you," Robin whispered the words into her ear.

The realisation that her body was responding automatically to Robin's touch gave Ellie the strength to pull herself together. Robin had trapped one of her legs between hers and she had to push hard to free herself.

"You think you do now." Ellie wiped at her eyes with her sleeve. "Do you really want me, or is it just that now you've seen the competition, you want a piece of the action?"

"God, Ellie, is that what you really think of me?"

"What have you ever done to make me feel any differently?"

Jo reached them then with the dog still struggling in her grasp. "I'll put him in the van."

*Jen Silver*

"Okay. I'll go and have a look at his discovery. Kathryn's on her way." Ellie walked off down the field leaving Robin staring after her.

✝

Jo shut a seriously annoyed Harry in the van, he was still grumbling as she closed the door in his face. Returning to where Robin stood watching Ellie's retreating back, it was obvious to her as the rank outsider that these two had some major issues to work out. She didn't regret the night she'd spent with Robin, it had been fun, but seeing her at the farm, she could tell there was a part of her that belonged here.

"What did she mean...about Kathryn? Hasn't she phoned the police?"

Robin turned to face her and Jo could see the strain in her face. "The bone may not be too recent. And Kathryn wants to dig up the field anyway; she thinks there's a Roman fort or something there. That's why she came last night."

"Holy Moly. You mean you could have your own *Time Team* right here?"

"Yeah. But I don't think Ellie's too thrilled about it."

"They'll have to call the cops anyway."

"Why?"

"Any crime novel I've ever read, if they find bones on a site they have to stop digging while the police bring in a forensic archaeologist who can determine how old the bones are. Anything within the last century and they'll have to start an investigation, find out who it is and what happened. And the dig gets shut down until the police say it can be reopened."

"Well, that will upset the professor. Her dig gets shut down before it's even started."

"Robin!" Jo decided to try and tease her out of her dark mood. "You needn't sound so pleased."

"Well, what does Ellie see in the stuck-up bitch, anyway?"

"Hm. Let me think. Intellectual, caring, not bad looking..."

"Piss off, Jo." This was said without animosity as Robin finally turned away from the field and looked at her. And for the first time that morning she smiled. "Want to collect the eggs for breakfast?"

"Absolutely. Lead me to the henhouse." Harry set up a long, drawn-out howl as they walked away from the van.

"Will he be all right?" asked Robin.

"Yes. He'll make a fuss for a bit. I'll give him some treats later, but he had breakfast not too long ago."

Jo matched Robin's long strides easily. She'd changed into jeans this morning, realising her long skirt was impractical for wearing around the farm. No, she didn't regret the night spent with Robin. And if there were a chance she and Ellie didn't get back together, she wouldn't mind another night or two of Robin's loving. Since Jules had left her high and dry at the Leeds Festival the previous year she'd decided long-term relationships weren't her scene. Harry had pitched up at just the right time, a woebegone stray. She'd felt much the same, abandoned by a woman she'd loved for more than two years. Jules had seemed to be the perfect partner, sharing the life of a traveller in the van, moving from town to town, going to music festivals and selling their wares at craft fairs. This had obviously just been a stopgap until she met another sucker, the smart-looking festival tourist who had taken Jules off to her luxury condo in Harrogate. Not so much as a backward glance from her now ex-lover.

Recently she'd been coming round to the idea of settling down and Hebden Bridge looked like the best option. It had a community feel, the type of community she could fit into, be accepted.

Her emotions had been at an extremely low ebb when she met Robin at the craft fair in the autumn. It was the two-month anniversary of Jules's defection. Meeting Robin had been a great lift. She made her laugh when they were on the stall together and at the end of the day she found she'd sold more than ever before. Jo didn't usually find herself attracted to androgynous-looking women like Robin but by the time they had finished packing up she found herself inviting her to spend the night.

†

The drive seemed to take forever. After collecting Ed from the university car park they had struggled through the early morning traffic to get out of town. Kathryn filled him in on the developments and the stage of her delicate negotiations with the prospective site's owner, Ellie Winters.

"I've tried to convince her that this could be more important than the fort they found a few miles from here at Slack. And that's mostly covered over by the golf course now. I just hope she'll agree to the dig," she concluded glumly.

"The bones might persuade her, if they are..." he left the sentence unfinished.

"If they are," she continued, "there will be a lot of media interest. This will be massive. Ellie won't be thrilled to find TV crews camped out on the farm." Kathryn caught him looking at her out of the corner of her eye. "What?"

"So, what exactly is your relationship with Miss Winters? Just so I don't put my foot in it." Ed was the only member of staff she had talked to about her intermittent sex life. Coming out to her colleagues wasn't something Kathryn had felt was necessary. A few of them probably guessed as she never brought a partner to staff parties or talked about children or grandchildren.

"We saw each other for a while, a few months, then it just sort of fizzled out."

"Until you found out she's sitting on previously undiscovered Roman remains. So, now you're screwing her again."

"Jesus, Ed! Leave it out. It's not like that at all."

"Right." He lapsed into silence, the early morning light reflecting off his glasses. After they had left the town behind and were climbing into the hills on a narrow country lane, crumbling dry stone walls marking out field boundaries on either side, she was startled by a loud guffaw from her colleague.

Risking a quick glance at him, the road had narrowed to one lane with no passing places, she asked, "What's so funny?"

"I get it now. I wondered why you bought this car. I mean you weren't due to get a new one for at least eighteen months." Ed knew she always bought a new car every three years, whether the car needed replacing or not.

"So?"

"So, in a man this kind of purchase would be called a penis extension. I don't know what the dyke equivalent is..."

Kathryn set her lips in a thin line. She wasn't going to rise to his teasing. "Let's just stick to business, please." Even without turning her head from the road in front of her, she could feel his smirk. She wasn't going to let him derail her mood.

Ever since hearing Ellie's voice on that early morning phone call, Kathryn had been in a heightened state of excitement. Postponing the regular Tuesday morning department meeting, her next call had been to Ed, and he'd been agreeable to putting off a day's worth of scrutinising the academic efforts of his second year MSc students to make the trip and take a look at the bone.

*Jen Silver*

"Sturnus Colle," she said as they turned up the track leading to the farm. "That would have been the Roman name for this place. Starling Hill."

"Hm." Ed was looking about him with interest. "I can see how this would be a good place for a fort. You'd think they would have built a better road, though."

"Oh. Good point. That's something else we'll need to look for. If she agrees, of course."

"Of course."

"What are you grinning at?"

"Nothing. I'm just looking forward to seeing you in action. This poor woman doesn't stand a chance."

"Very funny." She pulled into the yard, and it was only as she parked next to Jo's camper van and saw Ellie come out of the house followed by a decidedly scruffier-looking Robin, that she realised she hadn't filled Ed in on the ménage she had walked into the night before.

†

Kathryn arrived just as the three of them were finishing breakfast, each having managed a fresh double-yolker egg with toast and coffee. Jasmine and the young couple had still not surfaced. Jo jumped up to put more coffee on as Ellie went out to greet her visitors. Following slowly, Robin thought the professor looked like a retriever ready for a signal from her handler, itching to get at her prey. The man who climbed out of her car was a professor clone, tall, balding, glasses stuck on the end of his nose. Kathryn introduced him as Dr Ed McLaughlin, an expert on old bones.

"We've got coffee on, if you'd like some," said Ellie.

"Maybe later." Kathryn set off towards the field.

"She's keen," muttered Robin as she fell into step with the tall stranger.

58

"Very," he said equably.

Robin took another look at him. He seemed perfectly at ease strolling beside her with his hands in his pockets. "So, will you be able to tell how old this bone is, just by looking at it?"

"Not likely. We will need examine the context more closely and do some tests."

"Are you a professor doctor as well?"

"No, just doctor. Although a find like this will certainly help me move up the ladder if I can publish a decent academic paper on it."

"Is that why Kathryn's so excited? Kudos all round for her department and the university?"

"Partly. But she was already excited by the aerial survey photos. She just needs your friend to agree to have her life turned over as well as the turf in this field."

"Seems a bit cold-blooded."

"Archaeology can seem that way to the outsider. We sift through the rubbish left by our predecessors and try to work out how they lived...and died. The human condition, we're all affected some way or other."

They had reached the others now. Kathryn was crouching over the hole dug by Harry, staring at the protruding bone. She looked up as they approached. "I guess the teeth marks are from the dog. They look recent."

Ed squatted down beside her. "Hm. I don't suppose you've got any digging equipment with you, Kat? It would be useful to have a context."

"Don't we have to call the police?" asked Robin, mindful of Jo's words earlier.

"Not yet. A single unidentified bone isn't particularly useful. And it's too big to be a child's."

Robin shivered. She hadn't been born when the moors murders were headline news, but the continuing torment for the family of the body not found was never far from the headlines as she was growing up. Then Peter Sutcliffe's ripper rampage had brought the horrors of that time to the fore again.

"But the coroner will have to be informed," Ed continued. "Not sure why this bone has surfaced now if it's as old as we think it is." He turned to Ellie. "Has this field been ploughed?"

Ellie turned an empty gaze towards him. She shook her head. "It's only ever been used for grazing sheep."

"Do you still have sheep?" Ed asked, looking around at the short grass and evidence of sheep droppings.

"No, I sold them after my father died. But my neighbour, Owen Chappell, grazes his sheep here on and off through the year. Saves us having to mow it. His farm's over that ridge."

Kathryn stood up and threw her car keys to Robin. Startled, Robin just managed to catch them. "There's a shovel and trowels in the boot. Would you mind getting them?"

Robin looked over at Ellie, but she was staring off into the distance. "Okay." She guessed the professor wanted to talk to Ellie with her out of the way.

Jo came out of the house as she was removing the tools from Kathryn's car. "Do you think they'll want some coffee?"

"Yeah. Might as well make them feel at home. Looks like they're going to be here for a while. Anyone else up yet?"

"No, though I'm surprised Harry's howling hasn't woken them." They both turned to the van. Harry was looking out with his paws on the dashboard and making enough noise to wake the dead.

†

Ellie watched as Kathryn and Ed paced out a sizeable area. They were discussing the best way to approach what they were referring to as the find. Her ex-lover had taken her to one side after Robin went back to the car for the tools. "Are you okay with this?" she'd asked anxiously. Ellie had shrugged, not trusting herself to speak. It didn't feel like she was going to have much say in whether the dig took place or not. Kathryn continued to explain, "We just need to open a small trench here to see if there's more bones. Ed's very good, he'll be careful."

Robin arrived with the shovel and trowels. Taking in the size of the area the two academics had marked out, she offered to get another spade from the stables. Jo arrived with coffee after Robin had set off back up the field. Ellie was amazed to see she'd found everything, including a tray and a sugar bowl.

Ed took the tray from her and thanked her profusely. "Miss Winters," he said, addressing her formally. "Do you have any plastic bags we could use? I'm sorry to prevail on you like this, but my colleague here didn't give me much notice and I wasn't expecting to have to get my hands dirty."

Ellie gave him a small smile. "Please call me Ellie. You make me feel like an old spinster calling me Miss Winters. I'll go and get some bags."

"I'll go," said Jo.

"Thanks. They're under the sink." Ellie was surprised at the revelation of Jo's practical side coming to the fore. "Oh, and could you ask Robin to bring the folding table from the studio? And we might as well have some chairs as well."

The two archaeologists worked easily together. Robin helped remove the turf and a top layer of soil. Then Ed got down on his knees to scrape away with a trowel. Kathryn took photos with her phone's camera, making sure she covered all angles. Jo kept them all supplied with drinks and biscuits. Ellie just watched. She couldn't quite believe this was really happening. Sheep had grazed over this field for all the generations her family had lived on the farm. The terrain was uneven but that hadn't bothered the animals, as long as there was grass to munch.

Ellie was just thinking she was going to need to offer them lunch when Ed sat back on his heels and they all looked in wonder at the bones he had uncovered. "I'm sure there's a full-sized skeleton under here," he said. "These are from the lower end of the body, so I suspect we'll find a skull if we open the trench up that way." He indicated north with his trowel.

†

Jasmine rolled over again to check the time on her phone. Shit, it was later than she thought. Must've dozed off after waking up with the dawn chorus at four. Not for the first time since her arrival she wondered why anyone would choose to live here. Well, best get up and face the day. She had her work cut out for her. Robin was playing hard to get but Jas wasn't planning to give up easily.

Taking the towel Ellie had left her, she headed into the bathroom for a shower. Feeling more refreshed and dressed for action in a tight black skirt and crop top, which left nothing to the imagination, she made her way to the kitchen. No human life, just the large ginger cat staring at her from the top of the stove. It looked like there had been some breakfast-type activity though, dishes everywhere. Pouring herself a large glass of orange juice from the fridge, Jas took her drink outside.

Looked like the professor was back, the bright red car standing out against the backdrop of the grey stone of the stables. Narrowing her eyes against the strong sunlight, Jas could see movement in the field. She knocked back the remaining juice, set the cup on the edge of the step and walked across the yard to see what was happening.

Robin was leaning on a shovel, looking into a hole in the ground. The professor and a strange man were bending over the hole, intent on whatever was inside. Ellie and Jo were standing by a table that had an array of cups on it. The scene looked like the start of a Mad Hatter's tea party. Appropriate, thought Jas. They were all mad as hatters here.

She looked down at her feet. There was no way she could make it across the field in these fashion sandals. She called out and waved to get the group's attention. Robin looked over then quickly back into the hole. It was Jo who responded, picking up the tea tray and saying something to Ellie before moving towards her.

"What's going on?" Jas asked as soon as Jo was close enough to hear without her having to shout.

"Harry found a bone and Kathryn thinks there's a Roman fort under here. That's why she came to see Ellie yesterday." Jo was flushed with excitement.

Kathryn. Ooh, things were hotting up. "Who's the guy?"

"He's one of her colleagues, a bone specialist."

"Are they going to do a dig here?"

"Looks like it. I don't think Ellie's too thrilled, though. It will mean a lot of disruption."

Jas's PR mind clicked into gear. "But, this could be big. They haven't found anything like this around here before, have they?"

"I don't know, but Kathryn and this other boffin are certainly excited about what might be here. And they're expecting to find more bones from what I've seen them doing this morning..."

"Wow. Fantastic."

They were moving towards the house and as they neared the camper van, Harry started howling.

"Oh, damn. I forgot about poor Harry. Jasmine, could you take these into the kitchen? I need to see to him."

Jas nodded and took the tray from her without comment. She had other things on her mind.

†

Robin washed her hands. The academics had gone, taking some soil samples with them for testing but leaving the bones Ed had uncovered in place. The coroner had been informed and would be arriving later in the day to assess the situation. Using an old tarpaulin, they had covered up the area of disturbed ground in the field before leaving. Everyone else had gone too. Aiden and Sophie, having slept through the early morning excitement, hadn't surfaced until noon and then left quickly, as they both had to be at work the following day. Jo had decided it was best to remove Harry from the scene, as he was still distressed about not being able to have his bone. She promised Ellie she would be back later in the week to continue her pottery lesson. And Jas had taken off, after talking briefly with Kathryn.

It would be a relief to have the place to themselves for a bit and a chance to talk properly with Ellie. She'd been withdrawn during the digging session and discussions between Ed and Kathryn. Before leaving, Kathryn had taken her on one side. Robin hadn't been able to hear the conversation, just saw Ellie nodding before turning away and going into the studio.

"What was that about?" she'd asked Kathryn, arms folded across her chest.

The professor had given her what Robin thought of as her teacher-confronted-by-dimwitted-student look. Then she'd said calmly, "Nothing for you to worry about."

"I live here, too. So, it might be."

Kathryn shrugged. "She's agreed to the dig. I've told her we'll have a contract drawn up."

"That's reassuring. It'll turn her life upside-down."

"I'm aware of that. But I'll be here and will do what I can to minimise the disruption." With that, she'd walked back to her car where Ed was waiting.

Robin came out of the bathroom and went into the living room to find Ellie there, staring at the empty grate in the fireplace.

"Hey, El. You okay?" She moved towards her.

Ellie stopped her with a motion of her hand then turned around. Robin could see the worry lines deepening in her forehead.

"Ellie, love…"

"Stop. Don't."

"Don't, what?"

"I've had to make some hard decisions today and this one's the hardest." Ellie took a deep breath and then looked her in the eyes. "I want you to leave. It's not working, you being here. I thought I could handle it. But I can't…and now with this. Well, it's too much."

"Ellie, please. You don't mean it! I can help you. You'll need support."

"I have friends, real friends."

"Look. Jas has gone. I'm not interested in her. I want you. I want to be with you."

"And how often have I heard that from you? That's what you say you want, until the next one comes along."

"Ellie, please. It's different this time." Robin was rigid with the shock of Ellie's determined look.

"I've made up my mind Robin. Please…just go." Ellie pushed past her and ran upstairs. Robin heard the bedroom door slam, the stark reality of Ellie's words finally registering.

†

Ellie sat on the bed, taking deep breaths, trying not to hyperventilate. The events of the past twenty-four hours flashed before her eyes. How could her life change so drastically in that short span of time? The last few months had been hard enough. She thought she could cope with Robin being home again; and it had been comforting at first, just having her around. But then the remembrance of what they had shared for so many years would engulf her. The realisation that she wanted her back not just in the house, but also in her bed, was driving her to distraction. Robin exuded so much sexiness just by breathing. All she wanted was to feel her arms around her again, her warm breath on her neck, her hands feeling their way under her shirt, a mischievous grin playing over her face.

However, the feelings of betrayal were also very raw. And the presence at the farm of not just one, but two, of Robin's lovers had been hard to take. She knew she wasn't completely blameless. After all, she had given in to a few nights of lust with Kathryn.

She had agreed, as she knew she would, to Kathryn's request to organise a full-scale dig on what the professor was already referring to as the site. Seeing the outline of a skeleton emerge before her eyes had been disturbing. No matter that she avidly read archaeology magazines and pored over images from other places in the country where large numbers of skeletons from the same period had been found, she wasn't prepared for the feeling of dismay at the bones now unearthed on her land.

Finally, she heard Robin's motorcycle, a few revs and then she was gone, roaring down the track. The tears she'd been holding back all day started to flow. Ellie didn't know where she'd found the strength to go through with it, but she knew it was the right thing to do.

Part Two

# Chapter Four

## Preparations

Kieran Taylor drove up the farm lane wondering what he would find. Ellie had sounded strange on the phone. It had taken him a week to get over the jet lag on his return from Australia and he wondered if she was mad at him for not phoning sooner. But Ellie wasn't usually like that. He'd known her when she was Mrs Caffrey and had first come to him for pottery lessons. A shy woman, but incredibly talented. He often thought she undersold herself.

The farmhouse came into view and the familiar sight suddenly looked askew. What were those ugly things blocking the way to the field and the usually unrestricted scene of the wooded hillside in the distance? They looked like portable toilets. "WTF," as his son had taught him to say. *Eleanor Winters, what have you done?*

He had to park at the top of the lane. There was a line of vehicles parked along the length of the stables. No sign of the motorbike though. So, at least the alley cat wasn't in residence. Sighing, he ran his hand over his newly cropped hair. Ellie wouldn't recognise him. His son had told him the ponytailed look was outdated. He was never going to pull if he continued to look like an overage hippie. Tommy seemed to think he needed to find another woman to stave off lonely old age. He'd told him he wasn't lonely and anyway how would he ever find a woman to match Tommy's mother.

"Kieran!"

He looked up to see Ellie running towards him, surprised as she leapt at him. Not used to such an enthusiastic reception, he reacted automatically, wrapping his arms around the small woman. She was shaking. He held on to her, feeling her calm slowly.

"Well, I've missed you too. But I wasn't expecting that."

She looked up at him. He could see that her eyes were wet. "What have you done to your hair?"

"Tommy told me the 1960s was fifty years ago. Time to move on."

She smiled but the expression didn't reach her eyes.

"So, what's going on here?" he asked, gesturing towards the field.

"It's a university-sponsored dig. They think they've found a Roman fort or some kind of settlement here, including some skeletons."

"You're kidding!"

"No. And this is just the start. They're marking out the places they want to dig. By this time tomorrow we'll be overrun with eager students."

"Are you doing the catering?"

"No! And I've had to put my foot down about having a catering van onsite. The uni is providing packed lunches and thermos flasks. Hence, the loos as well. Anyway, come in and have a cup of tea."

Kieran followed her into the house. She busied herself, filling the kettle, getting out mugs, and sugar for him. He observed her movements. She had lost some weight and there wasn't a lot she could afford to lose. He hoped she wasn't ill. Having watched his wife deteriorate slowly, ravaged by lung cancer, he didn't think he could bear to see it again in someone he cared about. He remembered his son coming home from school suddenly enthused about history, a subject he'd never shown any interest in before, captivated by this inspiring young woman. And when he had finally met her at a parents' evening, he could understand his son's infatuation and would have liked to be thirteen again.

"How's Tommy?" she asked, as if reading his train of thought.

"Absolutely ecstatic at being a father, at last. Always was a late starter."

"I hope you've brought some photos."

"Of course." He pulled his phone out of his shirt pocket. Catching Ellie's look, he laughed. "One day, Miss Winters, you'll catch up to the twenty-first century."

She brought his mug to the table and sat down next to him. They looked at the pictures together.

"They look very happy," she said, gazing at the photo Maya's mother had taken of the four of them—Kieran holding the baby, the proud parents on either side of him. "Later this year, I should have some photos to show you."

"Aiden and Sophie. Great news. Are they getting married?"

"Not yet. I wonder if Aiden really knows what he's getting into. Fortunately Sophie has enough common sense for both of them."

"Yes." They lapsed into a companionable silence. Fleur had crept in and insinuated herself onto Kieran's lap. He stroked her absentmindedly. Whatever was eating at Ellie it wasn't anything to do with Aiden and Sophie, he was sure of that. "This dig," he ventured, "is the professor involved?"

Ellie gave him a small smile. "Yes, of course. She's in charge."

"Is it on again?" Kieran had hoped the affair with Dr Moss would last. She was, in his opinion, a better match for Ellie than the feckless Robin.

"No."

He put his hand over hers. "Ellie, I can see something's wrong. What is it?"

"I…" She shook her head, on the verge of tears again.

"Well, no prizes for guessing. It's Robin, isn't it?"

"I told her to leave. I thought I couldn't handle it, her being here. And now, I don't know where she is. No one's heard from her. Oh God, Kieran. Now I just want her back again."

"How long's she been gone?"

"Two weeks."

He stood up, displacing Fleur, who gave him a withering look before stalking off.

"Come here," he said to Ellie. She let him embrace her. He stroked her hair. "Robin's a survivor. She's probably holed up somewhere." He didn't add, with another woman.

Ellie cried on his shoulder for several minutes before managing to pull herself together.

"Look," he said as she dried her eyes. "I know it's hard at the moment. But you've done the right thing. You had to do it, for your own self-respect."

"Funny, that's exactly what Aiden said."

"See, the boy has some sense after all."

She smiled at that, but he could see the effort it took her to hold back more tears.

"So, are you going to show me this Roman encampment of yours," he said. "Tommy will be extremely jealous. And if he didn't have a newborn son, he'd be on the first plane over."

✝

Robin sat at the crossroads. One road led to Starling Hill, the other would take her, eventually, to the market town in the next valley. Could she blame Aiden for siding with his mother? Not really, but she had been counting on her usually strong relationship with him to at least be able to stay with them for a few weeks while she sorted herself out. She'd left the farm with only her backpack, filled mostly with electronic devices. She didn't have any clean clothes left.

With a sigh she turned away from the road leading to the farm. The ride into the neighbouring hills and across the moorland sweeping down into the Calder Valley was exhilarating and lifted her spirits. Surely she could expect a warmer welcome from Jo Bright Flame. It had taken all her self-control not to laugh out loud when Jo had given her full name when they first met. She'd managed to just smile and say, "Bright Flame?" It had been Jo's rebellion against her parents, she said. Dropping out of high school, having been moved around Europe as a child from army base to army base, she had taken to travelling on her own. And being called Jo Johnson didn't fit in with her new lifestyle. She wanted to shake off the JoJo tag she got stuck with during her schooldays.

Finding Jo was the problem now. She didn't have a phone number for her and Jo didn't have a fixed address. Robin headed for the marketplace. It was busy, another trading day, mainly fruit and vegetables this time. However a stall selling old CDs, DVDs, and comics looked a likely source of information. With her bike tucked in between two cars on the side road next to the market, Robin walked through the stalls and stopped to casually flip through the music selection. When the proprietor asked her if she was looking for anything in particular, Robin replied, "Actually, I'm looking for someone. Do you know Jo Bright Flame? She usually has a craft stall here?"

"Oh, that'll be on Wednesdays. You're a day late."

"Damn. She said I should look her up when I was passing through."

"Well, as it happens, I do know Jo." The man smiled, his teeth gleaming through his long greying beard. "She parks up by the Co-op when she can."

Robin nodded. She remembered where the Co-op was from her last visit, the only supermarket-style store the inhabitants of the town felt comfortable with. It wasn't far from the market. Thanking the man, she decided to leave her bike where it was and walk along the road by the river to find the colourful camper van.

†

Jo wasn't surprised to see Robin. She had visited the farm earlier in the week to arrange times to see Ellie about the pottery lessons. It was the day the portable loos were being delivered and Ellie was glad to see her. They had tea together and eventually Ellie asked if she had seen Robin. She seemed upset at not knowing where Robin was, but at the same time didn't seem to want her back.

When she opened the door of the van and found Robin standing there, motorcycle helmet dangling from one hand, she just said, "Wait there." Finding Harry's lead on the floor near the mattress she clipped it on the excited dog and joined Robin outside. "He needs a walk," she said. It was a lovely warm day and she had been thinking of taking Harry out. She led the way to the canal path. "There's a pub along here."

Neither of them spoke as they walked down the towpath. With no one else in sight, Jo let Harry off his lead and he leapt ahead joyously, sniffing everything and stopping occasionally to lift his leg. The pub had seating outside facing the canal. Jo secured an outside table, calling Harry to her, while Robin went to the bar to get their drinks. With the dog settled at their feet and pints of beer in front of them, they gazed at the water in silence.

Jo broke it first. "What's going on, Robin? I've seen Ellie. She doesn't know where you are."

73

"Why should she care? She doesn't want me there." Robin leant forward, elbows on the table, and placed her head in her hands.

"I don't think she knows what she wants. Maybe you just need to give her some space."

"There's enough sodding space on the farm. She didn't have to throw me out."

Jo stroked Harry's ears. "Obviously I don't know what's gone on with you two, but maybe she did. You have been screwing around, haven't you? I suspect Jas and I aren't the only ones."

"And what about her and the professor?"

"Well, can you blame her? You weren't there. Kathryn seems like a nice person. She probably just wanted the company."

"You can't tell me they weren't fucking."

"No. But I guess they would probably call it making love." Jo tried to keep the sarcasm out of her voice. Robin really did appear to be suffering.

"Thanks. Like I really needed to hear that."

"Robin, grow up!" This time Jo didn't hold back. "You say you want her, but you play the field. And you expect her to just sit at home and wait for you to come back. What kind of relationship is that?"

"I love her."

Jo looked at the woman next to her, body slumped, head in hands. She was crying. Putting a tentative hand on her shoulder she said, "Well, I think you've got a fair bit of work to do to convince her of that. It's going to take time."

"Fine." Robin sniffed. "In the meantime, where am I supposed to live?"

"I might be able to help you out there."

Robin looked up, the tears glistening on her cheeks. "No offence, Jo. But your van isn't big enough for a long-term arrangement."

"I don't mean the van. No, friends of mine need a house sitter. They're going to Canada for six months and don't want to leave it empty. It's a big house, and I won't be there all the time, so it would be good to have someone else around."

For the first time since arriving, Robin smiled. "Wow. That sounds ideal. When are you moving in?"

"Day after tomorrow."

"Great. So, can I bunk up with you tonight." She held up her hands. "No funny business, I promise."

"You'd be better off in a B&B."

"Do I smell?"

"Yes, you do a bit. Where have you been sleeping?"

"Crashed with a mate in Leeds for a few nights. I would have stayed longer but her girlfriend wasn't too happy with me being there."

"You didn't...?"

""Didn't what?" Robin looked at her and sighed, running her fingers through her short hair. "Oh, jeez, Jo. I'm trying to turn over a new leaf here. Anyway, I didn't fancy her." She attempted a grin but it looked more like a grimace.

They finished their beer in companionable silence. Jo enjoyed the peaceful environment of the canal, occasionally broken by passing cyclists, dog walkers, and ramblers. Robin, she suspected, was seeing a different scene in front of her eyes.

†

Kathryn arrived ahead of the coach that was bringing the students. She wanted to spend some time with Ellie explaining what would be happening. They hadn't been able to talk much in the weeks of preparation. Aside from the legal niceties that had to be taken care of, she was also juggling the university's admin requirements. This wasn't made any easier by the fact that the Human Resources department head had appointed Aimee Felton as their liaison. She and Aimee had history and hadn't parted amicably. Ed had laughed himself sick when he heard. "Oh, what fun. Wait until AF meets the delectable Miss Winters."

"For an academic, you have a salacious turn of phrase. Anyway, I can handle it."

"Of course you can." He smirked.

The report on the bone found by Harry revealed it to be easily first or early second century. The coroner had only made a cursory visit and assured them skeletons of that age were of no interest to the law. Kathryn was hoping that future finds on the site would help date it more accurately to on or around AD 120. This was the time when the Roman Army moved most of its troops north to start work on Hadrian's Wall. It still wasn't clear why there would have been a fort, or even a settlement, here at all. It wasn't on the main route between the two main legionary fortresses in northern England, Chester and York.

Breathing in the clear early morning air, Kathryn stood beside her car appreciating the stillness of her surroundings. Swallows swooped in the field, dipping gracefully to their own internal rhythms. The name of the farm was a mystery as she had yet to see the eponymous starling anywhere in the vicinity.

The constant whirring sound in the background gradually entered her consciousness. Taking in one last deep breath, Kathryn squared her shoulders and walked the short distance to the stables.

Ellie was intent on the moving clay in her hands. Kathryn watched, transfixed, and remembered those hands moving down the length of her body and the look of intensity on Ellie's face. She had enjoyed their lovemaking and wondered again why she had let this one get away. Was she so incapable of maintaining a loving relationship? The concentrated gaze on Ellie's features as she expertly maneuvered the rotating clay into a shape, Kathryn wouldn't mind inspiring that look in her direction. But in the last few weeks she had noticed the growing sadness in Ellie. She didn't know if it was because of the disruption to her life that the preparations for the dig were already causing. Or was it about the absent Robin?

Gradually the wheel slowed and Kathryn could see the shape of the object in Ellie's hands. It looked like a bowl, not so different from the remnants they would unearth in the weeks ahead. Finally, Ellie stopped the wheel and looked up at her. Kathryn wanted badly to walk over and gently move the stray strands of golden hair away from her face and take that face in her own hands and kiss her. Smooth away the unhappiness with gentle caresses.

Telling herself to get a grip, she cleared her throat. "The students will be arriving in about an hour. Do you want to be present when I address them?"

"Do I need to be?"

"It might be useful for them to know who you are. You're more than welcome to join us at any time. Or, just to come and watch. Anyway, I'll be telling them the ground rules, letting them know the farmhouse, hens, stables are all strictly out of bounds. They only have access to the field and the toilets. We've provided bins so there should be no litter. We'll also be putting up a tent today, for shelter and also for storing the finds initially. I'll personally check the site at the end of each day to make sure nothing's left out either in terms of rubbish or tools."

"Kathryn," Ellie held out a clay-covered hand, "I'm sure it will be fine."

"Okay. I'm just aware that this is a major imposition on your space here. The kids, well, they're young adults really, have also been told they can listen to their iPods or whatever, but only with earphones. No loud music blaring away. And they'll only be here from nine thirty to four thirty Monday to Friday."

"Good. I'll just wash my hands. Then what I would really like is to take a walk around the field and you can tell me what you'll be doing today."

†

Ellie took in the tranquility of the scene, a last lingering look. The coach was on its way up the track and Kathryn had gone to meet it. In a few moments her peace would be shattered, possibly forever. There wouldn't be much excavation work today. The morning was mainly a training session for the students. The top layer of turf had already been removed from the trenches they planned to look at first. That had turned up a few coins and potsherds. The coins, even without needing to be cleaned, Kathryn was sure showed the Emperor Hadrian's likeness on one side. Hadrian was always depicted with a beard, whereas his predecessor, Trajan was clean-shaven.

She glanced over at the theodolite set up on its tripod, the position fixed. Kathryn had explained that all the significant finds would be measured with the device. The entire site would be mapped out on her computer by the time they were finished.

Part of her was excited about the project, but at night, alone with her thoughts Ellie despaired. She was afraid of getting old, being alone. Aiden and Sophie had busy lives and she didn't want to be a burden to them. She knew what it was like to look after an ailing parent. The fear of being alone in her old age, was that a good enough reason for continuing a relationship with anyone, let alone someone like Robin?

And yet it was Robin who was continually in her thoughts. It was Robin she wanted to wake up with, to hold, to love, to laugh with. They used to laugh a lot. Where was she? Aiden had told her Robin came to see them two days after she'd left the farm. She had wanted to know if she could stay with them for a bit. But Aiden had said no, he was supporting his mother this time. It touched her that he had done that. He and Robin had always been so close. She could have phoned, but even the thought of hearing Robin's voice disturbed her. There were things she wanted to say, but she didn't know if she would be able to say them.

The sounds of the large vehicle arriving in the yard roused her from her melancholy thoughts. Time to face the reality of the day. She turned to observe the crowd now coming through the gate. Kathryn had said there was a fairly even gender split. Although, thought Ellie, with what some of them were wearing it was hard to tell the difference. Another old lady thought. She needed to lighten up if she was going to get through this with her sanity intact. Kieran had said he would look in today. He had some pots to fire, but she thought he was actually checking up on the visitors. Still, it was nice to have someone looking out for her interests.

Kathryn had organised the group. They were all standing in various poses, some fiddling with their music players and dangling earbuds; others were looking around with varying degrees of interest. She moved to stand next to Kathryn for the introduction. Then they separated into pre-arranged groups with two other staff members who were helping with the excavation.

After watching for a few minutes while the instructors passed around tools and explained how to use them, Ellie returned to the stables. Later in the morning she took a break and came face-to-face with Ed McLaughlin in the yard. He was struggling with a collection of tent poles.

"Hi. Can I help?"

He looked up and smiled at her. "It's okay. I'll just need to make several trips."

"Well at least let me carry something."

"Right. Could you grab the tent pegs?"

She had collected the pegs and they were starting off towards the field when Ed stopped and looked at the car pulling up next to his own. "Uh-oh. Didn't know she was coming today. This could be interesting."

Ellie looked over and saw a dark-haired young woman emerge from the driver's side of the vehicle. Her hair was tied back in a ponytail and she was dressed in tight-fitting jeans and knee-high leather boots, more elegant than necessary for a farm visit. It was the crop-top T-shirt, though, that drew the eye—and what was barely covered. Ellie wasn't sure but she thought she heard Ed stifling a giggle.

"Ed! Guess I'm in the right place. Just came to see everyone's turned up."

"Oh. Good. Well, walk this way. Aimee, this is Eleanor Winters, the owner of the farm. Eleanor, this is Aimee Felton, from the university's HR department. It's her job to make sure the students are being well treated, isn't that right, Aimee?"

"Sure thing. Kathryn's quite the slave-driver."

Ellie thought she heard a possessive tone in the words. Well, she hadn't thought Kathryn lived like a nun, but this was a revelation. If she liked them this young, why had she bothered with her?

The three of them made their way to the field. She followed Ed to the spot where he'd deposited the other parts of the gazebo. Aimee stalked off in Kathryn's direction. Ellie looked up to find Ed watching her.

"She's something else, isn't she?" he said.

"Yes. I wouldn't have thought she was Kathryn's type."

"No. I don't think Kathryn thinks that either. It was probably a mistake."

Ellie smiled tightly. "Well, we all make mistakes." She closed her eyes against the sun. What was her mistake?

Telling Robin to leave, and then wishing she hadn't? Or, not pursuing Kathryn when she had the chance? What did she want?

"Are you okay?"

"Yes, I'm fine. Look, my friend Kieran's coming over in a bit. He could help you put this thing up."

Ed grinned at her. "Do I look like a hopeless academic? No, don't answer that. I would welcome his help."

✝

The sight of Aimee striding across the field towards her, stopped Kathryn in midflow. She had been showing one of the boys how to take the top layer of soil off with care. She smiled at him. "You carry on, Patrick. I just need to talk to Ms Felton."

She met her before she reached the trench. "Is this really necessary, Aimee? I assure you I can count. The students are all present and correct."

"Of course they are, Kat. I just fancied a trip out of the office. You are pleased to see me, aren't you?"

"Don't call me Kat."

Aimee ignored her words and smiled broadly. "I think I might have to check up on you every day. Lovely spot here. I'll bring a picnic next time."

"This is work, Aimee."

"Looks like fun. Scratching about in the dirt."

"Aimee. I have got work to do."

"Of course. Does that include comparing notes with the farmer's wife?"

"If you mean Eleanor Winters, she's the sole owner of the farm."

"Oh. Well, I was wondering how you came across this site. Very convenient."

Kathryn willed herself not to respond to Aimee's caustic tone.

"Can she cook, too?"

"Aimee, if you've done your head count, then I think you should leave us to get on with it."

Whatever Aimee was going to say was drowned out with a shout. "Dr Moss! Over here, quick."

Kathryn looked over at the student now clamouring for attention. She moved quickly to his side.

"Look. There's something here. What do I do now?"

A sliver of a brown object showed through the partially disturbed earth, a slightly different shade. Another bone or a bit of pottery, it was hard to tell. Kathryn congratulated the student on his sharp eyes. "Stay there. I'll need to get some tools." Fetching several brushes and picks from her bag, she stopped to talk to Ed, who was looking at his collection of tent poles with some dismay. "Ed, one of the boys has found something. It may be another bone. Can you do me a favour and get her out of here?"

Ed didn't need to be told whom she was referring to. "Of course. But you'll owe me one."

"By the way, do you know how to put that thing up?" she asked as they hurried back down the field.

"Not yet. One of Eleanor's friends is coming to help, though."

"Who's that, then?" Kathryn asked.

"Guy called Kieran."

Kathryn felt relief. She had hoped it wouldn't be the ex-lover, Robin. And she was fairly certain Robin was definitely of the ex-status now. She did have some comparing notes to do with Ellie, but not anything to do with the dig.

†

Harry ran around the garden and marked out his new territory with enthusiasm. Jo had just waved goodbye to Wade and Ian. She'd met the pair at various festivals and craft fairs over the years and they always enjoyed a good time when they got together. Their decision to settle in this valley had been the main reason she had decided to try and put down some roots.

When she told them Robin would be moving in as well they thought it was good that she had company. Even with Harry's presence, it was a large house to rattle around in on one's own. Having taken in all their instructions and reassured them she knew whom to call in case of emergencies, she saw them load their luggage into the waiting taxi and told them not to frighten the lumberjacks.

It only took three trips to move her belongings from the van to the house. She decided to lay claim to the master bedroom with its king-sized bed and en suite bathroom. There were still three other bedrooms for Robin to choose from. The boys were excellent housekeepers. It would be difficult to maintain their high standard for six months. She doubted that Robin would be very handy with a hoover or a duster. The best option would be to pool their resources mid-January and hire professional cleaners to make sure the house was in pristine condition when the owners returned.

The sound of a motorbike reached her ears then. Leaning out of the bedroom window, she watched Robin park up next to the van and dismount. Then Harry appeared and jumped up to lick her face as soon as she removed her helmet. Jo made her way downstairs and went out to meet her new housemate.

"So, what do you think?" she asked.

Robin was looking around in wonder. "Wow! This is amazing. What do these two guys do? Did they win the lottery?"

"No!" Jo laughed. "Wade's an accountant and Ian does something with computers."

"So what are they doing in Canada for six months?"

"Seems they decided to have a half-year sabbatical. They have friends over there and they're just going to do a lot of things they've always wanted to do. Hiking through uncharted territory, canoeing, camping, and skiing in the Rockies. I don't know, sounded mad to me."

"Well, good for them. And for us. This place is fantastic."

"Yes. And you haven't seen the pool yet."

"There's a pool?"

"And a hot tub."

"Guess we'll survive then." Robin opened her saddlebag. "I did some grocery shopping. A few staples and beer, of course."

"Great. I was going to do that later."

"So, I'm not a total loser, then."

"I never said you were, Robin. Just a total fuck-up."

Robin looked at her, and for a brief moment Jo thought she had pushed her too far. Then Robin grinned, and they both started laughing.

†

"Where did you learn how to do this?" Ed asked, looking in admiration at the newly erected tent as Kieran knocked the last peg in.

Kieran smiled at him. *Academics, and what are they good for?* "Used to go on camping holidays when my lad was young."

"Well, thanks. It would have taken me a lot longer and then it would probably have collapsed with the first puff of wind."

"Fancy a beer?"

"Yeah, that would be good." It was a hot day and even though Kieran had done most of the work, Ed was perspiring. Kieran nodded and set off towards the house.

Ed followed slowly. "Hey. I thought the house was off limits."

"I'm sure Ellie won't mind. Promise not to trash the place."

Kieran opened two beers and set one down in front of Ed. The kitchen was the coolest room in the house during the day, helped by the natural slate floor tiles and the north-facing windows. Soames was dozing on one of the ledges and only opened one eye when they came in.

"Thought you'd be down in the field, looking at the bones they've found," Kieran said.

"It's going to take a while to remove enough soil for me to get a proper look. Kathryn will take every precaution and she has one of the students photographing all angles. I'd rather not be in the way."

Kieran nodded and sipped at his beer. He regarded the other man and decided he might as well ask. He was concerned for his friend. "Look, Doctor..."

"Please, call me Ed."

"Okay, Ed. I was wondering. Is there anything going on between Kathryn and Ellie?"

"Well, there was, but I think it ended a few months ago. However, that doesn't mean Kathryn's not interested. I've seen the way she looks at Eleanor."

Kieran smiled at Ed's use of Ellie's full name. She hated being called Eleanor, saying it made her feel old. If he were a few years younger, if she weren't gay, well there was no use dwelling on what wasn't going to happen. Ellie, at fifty-three, was easily the most attractive woman of his acquaintance. If Tommy wanted a stepmother, and if Ellie were available, he would have asked her to fill that place years ago.

"Anyway, isn't Eleanor still with that other woman? Tall with short, reddish brown hair. She was here the first time we came up to look at the site and was very helpful."

"Robin." Kieran grimaced as he said the name. "Ellie finally kicked her out."

"Oh. Why?"

"Why not, is a better question? Robin's messed her around for years. So, if Kathryn really is interested now would be the time to press her suit."

"And who's the one with the hippie van? I haven't figured out where she fits in."

"That's Jo. She wants to be a potter. So Ellie's giving her lessons." Kieran hadn't met Jo yet, but Ellie had mentioned her.

Ed nodded, curiosity satisfied, and finished off his beer. "Thanks for your help, Kieran. I'd better get back to the action before the boss sends out a search party."

✝

Robin set up her laptop in the dining room. She had two design commissions to work on. And she was glad to have something to take her mind off what was happening at Starling Hill farm and Ellie. Jo was visiting once a week but she forced herself not to ask. It was too painful. She didn't want to hear that Ellie was managing well without her, or worse, that the professor had got her feet firmly under the table again.

Living rent-free helped with her dwindling finances, but they still had day-to-day living expenses. Even with the money she would get from the completed artwork, she knew the time was coming when she would have to think about either getting a proper job or selling the bike.

Sitting and staring at the screen wasn't helping to move either project forward. Jo was at the farm and wouldn't be back until the evening. The only thing she'd managed to produce over the last few days was a letter to Ellie, which would never be sent. And that, she realised, was using up all her creative energy. Whatever she said, whichever way she said it, Ellie wasn't going to believe she had changed in the few weeks they had been apart. It may be that actions speak louder than words but what actions could she do that would convince the woman she loved that she was sincere? There were a lot of actions she would like to undo. Letting Jas invite herself to visit the farm was one of them.

Jasmine Pepper. How had she let herself get so involved? Seeing her out of the city context, she had realised that she didn't even really like her. It had just been a lust-filled interlude, like so many of her lapses. She loved women, and found it hard to resist an enticing encounter with any woman who looked at her twice. No wonder Ellie was upset. Why would she put up with that? Ellie was extremely attractive and offered more than enough to satisfy her libido.

Closing the laptop decisively, Robin thought she might as well take Harry for a walk. Jo had left him with her, as the number of people at the farm would only get him overexcited. Harry had been sleeping at her feet but he moved quickly when he realised she was getting his lead from the peg by the front door.

# Chapter Five

## Excavations

Jo breathed deeply as she climbed down from the van. Another fine day. The diggers were lucky this summer was so different from the ones of the last few years; otherwise they would have been knee-deep in mud by now. The pottery lessons were progressing well. Ellie had promised to show her how to mix the glazes today, and then she would be ready to fire her first pot. Well, it was a vase really. She had been planning to make a bowl, but somehow it had ended up a bit taller. Ellie had kindly told her it would pass as an old-fashioned drinking goblet without a handle. She assured her that control over the clay would come with practice.

The field seemed to be empty of excavators but then she saw that they were all crowded around one trench. It looked to be the same area where Harry had found the first bone. Checking first that Ellie wasn't waiting for her in the studio, she headed down to find out what they were looking at.

Spotting Ellie at the back of the crowd, she walked up to her and asked, "What's happening?"

"Yesterday, they uncovered a full skeleton. Now, it seems they've found another one."

"Gosh. That's amazing. To think they've been here all these years."

"Yeah. Amazing." Ellie's tone was flat.

Jo looked at her. "I thought you'd be thrilled by all this."

"I would be. If it wasn't here. In my field."

Kathryn emerged from the crowd just then. Her face was animated, flushed. "Ellie. Good, I need to talk to you. Let's go up to the house."

Jo followed at a discreet distance. She sensed that Kathryn didn't want her around but she thought Ellie might need support. She caught up with them as they entered the house. "I'll make some tea," she said.

Kathryn turned to look at her then. "This is a private conversation."

"I'd like Jo to stay. And tea would be lovely. Thanks, Jo." Ellie sat down at the kitchen table giving Kathryn no choice.

"Fine." Kathryn sat down as well.

Jo put the kettle on. She was familiar with the farm's kitchen by now and quickly found all the necessary items. The silence lengthened as neither of the other women spoke until the tea was ready and they were all sitting with mugs in front of them. Ellie broke the silence first.

"So, what do you want to talk to me about?"

"This find. We think there are more bodies. It's important to know what was going on here. At the moment we don't know if it is a burial ground or a place of rituals."

"You mean like human sacrifice?" Jo asked.

Kathryn looked at Jo for the first time. "Yes. That's a possibility."

"And what does that mean?"

"It means we need to open more trenches. I'm sorry, Ellie. It also means there may be some publicity."

"I thought we agreed that wouldn't happen until you were finished."

"I know. But, this is bigger than we expected. There are a lot of questions needing answers. The stonework we've uncovered suggests Roman influence, but it's not quite Roman standard. And those gold coins I showed you the other day are not Roman. We're going to need to bring in more people with expertise. And, I'm afraid, news has leaked out."

Ellie took a sip of her tea and looked towards the window, angling her body away from Kathryn. Jo thought the silence would go on forever until finally Ellie looked back at the professor. "How?" she asked quietly.

Kathryn looked confused. "How, what?"

"How has the news leaked out?"

"I'm not sure. I've talked with all the staff and students. They all say they've been discreet, even with close friends and family. From the outset they were advised, if asked, to say it was just an exercise to help them with their coursework. And I believe them. It has to be external. I was contacted personally by a reporter from one of the national papers."

"So. Didn't you tell them it's just an exercise?"

"I tried. But they said they had information telling them it was an important archaeological find."

"Jasmine," said Jo suddenly. The other two women looked at her. "Well, she was here the morning Harry discovered the bone. I always wondered why she left so quickly. It wasn't just because Robin was ignoring her." As soon as she mentioned Robin's name she wished she hadn't. But Ellie didn't react as she expected.

"Of course. Jasmine's in public relations. It would be just like her. She probably expects to make some money out of this."

Kathryn had brightened up. "Yes, you're right. I knew it couldn't be one of the team."

"All right." Ellie seemed calm. "But how are you going to handle it? I don't want the place crawling with paparazzi or treasure hunters with metal detectors. The site is so open."

"I'll talk to Ed. We'll come up with something. Don't worry." Giving Jo a look that clearly said she was in the way, Kathryn stood up to leave. "I'd best get back."

Jo took Kathryn's mug to the sink, and then poured out more tea for herself and Ellie, who was staring into space again. Suddenly she jumped up and ran out of the room. Thinking she'd gone after the professor, Jo stayed where she was and sipped her tea.

It was only a matter of moments, though, before Ellie was back. She sank into her chair and looked bleakly at Jo. "'An important archaeological find.' Jasmine didn't know if the bone held any significance. But several of the aerial photos Kathryn gave me are gone."

"That's all she would need, then, to convince a reporter that the site is of interest."

"Exactly. The cow!"

"Look, I know it's worrying, but I'm sure Kathryn will sort it out. It's in her interests to keep the site safe."

"Yes, well, it's all about her interests, isn't it?"

Jo put one of her hands over Ellie's. "I know she'll do what she can. She cares about you, too."

"Do you think so?"

"I've seen the way she looks at you. And you like her, don't you?"

Ellie's face took on the faraway look that Jo had seen so often on her recent visits. Pushing back her chair she stood up abruptly. "Time to have a look at those glazes. The pots won't fire themselves."

Subject closed. Jo knew she wouldn't get anything more out of Ellie on that front. It might be worth pursuing at a different time though. Much as she liked Robin, she thought Kathryn and Ellie would be a better match.

†

Having seen the students off the premises, packed up the theodolite equipment and the day's finds, Kathryn waited by her car. She knew that Ellie and Jo were still in the pottery studio. Jo's brightly painted camper van was parked in the yard and she could hear their voices through the open studio door.

Shoving her dirt-encrusted hands into the pockets of her sand-coloured shorts, she waited. Ed had offered to talk to the dean about the publicity issue, so that was one less problem for her to worry about. He thought the university would be able to provide some security. Usually her evenings involved taking the recorded finds back to her lab at the university and updating the data on the computer. And her week didn't end once the students left on a Friday evening. Saturdays she spent washing and sorting the other finds, putting them in carefully labeled trays to dry. The coins and stamped pottery shards had helped date the site to the Hadrianic era. As they uncovered more layers, there was evidence of earlier occupation as well. The Celtic finds unearthed the previous week she had couriered to the British Museum for analysis with another theory of who had occupied the site forming in her mind.

The two women emerged from the studio just as she was thinking she would have to wait another day to get Ellie on her own. Jo was carrying a large piece of colourfully glazed pottery and looked pleased. Ellie stopped short when she saw Kathryn.

"Everyone's gone for the day. But I would really like to talk to you."

"Okay." Ellie swiped at a stray strand of hair. Her face was streaked with sweat and Kathryn thought she had never looked more appealing. "I'll just get cleaned up." Turning to Jo, she said, "See you on Thursday."

"Yeah. And thanks. Today was fantastic."

Ellie just nodded and set off towards the house.

Kathryn looked at Jo, willing her to take off as quickly as possible, but the woman was standing there grinning inanely. "What is that, by the way?" she asked, looking at the object in Jo's hands.

"It was meant to be a bowl, but it sort of turned into a vase. Ellie says it will take time to get a feel for the clay."

"You don't have any designs on Ellie, do you?"

Jo looked at her, puzzled for a moment before the penny dropped. "Oh. You mean...no. I like her, obviously. And she's a great teacher."

"And what about Robin? Does Ellie talk about her?"

"No. But I think she misses her."

"Who would miss a cretin like that? I mean, she cheated on her all the time, didn't she?"

"Yes, but they were together a long time. It seemed to work for them." Jo looked uncomfortable with Kathryn's line of questioning.

"Okay. Well, I don't want to keep you." Kathryn set off towards the house.

Ellie wasn't in the kitchen or the living room so she went into the downstairs loo to wash her hands. Her hair was in need of a good brush, but it would have to do. Ellie knew what she looked like first thing in the morning and this wasn't any worse. Giving herself an encouraging smile in the mirror, Kathryn straightened her shoulders and went out to look for the woman she was trying to woo.

She found Ellie in the kitchen opening a bottle of wine. Just the job for unwinding at the end of a day in the field. And making a proposal.

"Hey." She announced her presence. "Do you need help with that?"

"Thanks. I've got it." Ellie didn't seem surprised by her sudden appearance. "The glasses are in the cupboard next to the sink."

"You had a long session with your apprentice."

"Well, she's keen."

"I'll say. I thought she was only coming once a week."

"She wanted to get in a few more sessions before the Leeds Festival. And Wednesdays she has a market stall." Ellie poured out the wine and handed a glass to Kathryn. "Anyway, I don't think you came in to talk about Jo."

"No." Kathryn took a sip of the wine and smiled. "Could we go and sit somewhere more comfortable? I've been on my knees for most of the day."

Once they were settled in the living room, Ellie in her favourite chair and Kathryn on the sofa, it took a few more gulps of wine before Kathryn felt able to speak.

"Ellie, I'm really sorry about the way things are going. I know you're finding this difficult."

Ellie just nodded and sipped her wine. Despite the fact that she was bone tired, literally, from the day's digging, Kathryn could feel her hormones rising. The heat between her legs was difficult to ignore. She recrossed her legs and tried to calm her breathing.

"I thought, maybe, you might like to get away for the evening. Have dinner out somewhere. There's that wine bar in Marsden we talked about going to before."

"Are you trying to soften me up, Professor? Do you have more bad news?"

"Not at all. It's just I've been so busy with this, we haven't had any time to talk."

"We're talking now."

"Ellie, please. Just say yes."

"Do you want to go like that?"

Kathryn looked down at her sweat-soaked T-shirt and grubby shorts. "I have a change of clothes in the car."

"Okay." Ellie drained the rest of her wine. "I can be ready in ten minutes. Do we need to book?"

"I'll ring them. But it should be okay on a Tuesday evening."

"Fine. I'll go get changed."

Kathryn smiled as she watched Ellie uncurl herself from the comfort of her armchair and run up the stairs. Perhaps this would be easier than she had thought. Maybe she was knocking at an open door.

†

Unsure what to wear for this unexpected outing, Ellie finally opted for her one pair of skinny leg grey jeans that would have been a tight fit a few weeks earlier. Still, they didn't look too baggy in the seat. She didn't have many blouses to choose from. Her wardrobe consisted mainly of old tees and sweatshirts. The blue shirt she found that was wrinkle-free was one Robin had bought her a few birthdays ago. The colour matched her eyes and they had been late for their restaurant booking, as Robin had immediately wanted to make love to her when she walked down the stairs.

Was she trying to seduce Kathryn, she wondered, leaving the top two buttons open to reveal the top of her lacy bra? Dabbing some perfume behind her ears, she decided that maybe she was. After all, Kathryn was the last person she had slept with, and that was five months ago now.

Kathryn had changed into loose-fitting cream chinos and a tailored white shirt. And she had brushed her hair, looking more presentable than she had ten minutes earlier. *Did she always carry a change of clothes with her?*

"We'll take my car," she announced when Ellie appeared.

"The Jeep would be more practical."

"My car's getting used to the humps and bumps. Come along, Cinderella, your chariot awaits."

Ellie let Kathryn take her arm as they walked out to the car. She decided this outing was a good idea, after all. They didn't talk during the drive, although Ellie thought it was unusual for Kathryn to stay silent for so long. They had conversed naturally when they were seeing each other before. Ellie drifted off, the road was all too familiar to her. It wasn't until Kathryn turned into the car park of a squat grey building by the roadside that she came to life.

"Hang on. I thought we were going to the bistro in Marsden."

"They couldn't fit us in and this place is owned by the same people."

Ellie couldn't see Kathryn's face but she doubted this was the truth. The restaurant they were now sitting outside was one of the top ones in the area. "Kathryn, I can't afford to eat here."

"Well, that's all right. It's my treat." She was getting out of the car, so Ellie followed, still protesting.

"Kathryn, if I'd known we were coming here I would have put something smarter on. I feel underdressed."

"You look fine." Kathryn tucked her hand under Ellie's elbow and steered her towards the entrance. At the doorway, Ellie stopped and planted her feet, forcing Kathryn to look at her.

"You planned this."

Kathryn gave her one of her enigmatic smiles. "Yes. Guilty as charged." Leaning in, she pulled Ellie close and gave her a quick kiss on the cheek before whispering in her ear, "Please. I just want to do something nice for you."

Ellie could feel the heat from Kathryn's lips on her earlobe and the tender skin of her neck. "Okay." She breathed out slowly. Kathryn let go of her and they walked into the welcoming atmosphere of the restaurant. Once they were seated and looking at the menu, Ellie let herself relax. She wasn't the worst dressed person there. Kathryn ordered a bottle of Sancerre, which Ellie knew without looking was one of the highest priced on the menu. It wasn't hard to guess what the professor wanted from her, and it wasn't a discussion on how the dig was going or how they were planning to maintain security of the site. She wasn't sure if she wanted the same thing, but it was nice to be wined and dined in style.

After they had ordered, their conversation settled into fairly mundane topics, starting with the weather and progressing to current affairs. By the time they were on the main course they had more or less set the world to rights. Her grilled sea bass was divine, and Kathryn seemed to be enjoying her Dover sole when she looked up and asked, "Have you ever thought about going back into teaching?"

Ellie put her fork down. "Where did that come from?"

"Your friend, Kieran. He told Ed that you were a wonderful teacher. Truly inspirational, I believe were his words."

"I couldn't go back to it now. I'm used to being my own boss. It's all changed so much in the last twenty years. Anyway, I would have to go back to uni and get a PGCE certificate. And I don't think history teachers are much in demand now. Everyone wants to do media studies or expressive arts."

"Well, I agree. You wouldn't want to go back to secondary education, but what about tertiary. I mean, higher ed."

"I know what tertiary means." Ellie pushed the last bit of fish around her plate. "But, no, I really haven't thought about it."

"But you're good with the kids. The students on the site love you. They're still raving about the pottery session you did for us last week."

"I've only spoken to a few of them." On her infrequent visits to the field to have a look at the progress in the trenches, Ellie often found herself approached by one or more of the youngsters. And after the pottery class Kathryn had talked her into giving when the dig was rained off one afternoon, they thought she was an authority on all things Roman.

Kathryn was smiling at her, mischievously. "And they think you're really fit."

"And that's a prerequisite for teaching nowadays, is it?"

"It helps."

Ellie sipped at the last of her wine and regarded Kathryn over the rim of her glass. The professor was definitely flirting with her. "I don't think I could manage dessert. But I wouldn't mind a coffee."

"Subtle change of subject, Miss Winters."

"You shouldn't try to embarrass me, Doctor Professor Moss."

"Touché."

✝

"I give up, Jo. What is it?"

"I'm heartbroken, Rob. I've spent two days creating this."

"Maybe you should stick to making those dangly things."

"Dream catchers. And don't mock. They put food on the table."

Robin looked at Jo and wondered if she could ask. Returning from a day at the farm, Jo was glowing. A day in Ellie's company, who wouldn't be?

"Anyway, I thought we should go out and celebrate."

"Celebrate what?"

"My first vase." Jo was cradling her creation in her arms.

"Oh, vase. Of course, I see it now."

"So, do you want to come?"

"Where?"

"A few of my mates will be at the Old Gate tonight."

"I don't know."

98

"Come on, Rob. You can't mope about here forever."

The last thing Robin felt like doing was going out to a noisy pub, but after a few more minutes of Jo's entreaties, she gave in. It was another beautiful summer's evening and telling Harry they would be back soon, they made their way down the steps of the narrow ginnel next to the house. Ten minutes leisurely walk brought them into the town centre. They crossed over the bridge to the large pub on the corner. Groups of smokers were gathered outside and they had to push their way through to get to the bar inside. Jo immediately saw someone she knew so Robin ordered the drinks. It was a struggle to fight her way back through the crowd to find Jo. The noise levels were already making it impossible to have a conversation without shouting. Handing Jo her bottle of Corona, Robin fought her way back outside. She hadn't smoked for many years, but now wished she had a cigarette. At least, as a prop. The first gulps of beer helped calm her nerves.

"Hey, haven't seen you around, before."

Robin turned to look at the speaker, a sporty-looking woman with hennaed hair, the red streaks glinting in the early evening sunlight. "Yeah, I'm new in town."

"Oh. I thought I saw you come in with Jo Bright Flame."

"She's my housemate." It seemed like a good idea to establish their relationship, or lack of it.

"So, do you make things as well?"

"No. I design websites and CD covers, that kind of thing. What about you?"

"I run a boxing gym."

"Really."

"Yeah. It's great exercise for all ages. You should try it. We have a women only class on Friday mornings. Jo knows where it is if you want to come along."

"Thanks. I'm Robin, by the way."

"Michelle."

Robin talked to Michelle for a bit longer before deciding she couldn't face going back into the noisy bear pit inside. Putting her empty bottle on a nearby table she asked Michelle to let Jo know she was heading out for a walk.

It was quieter down by the river and she found a place to sit where the stones were still warmed by the sun. Having lived on top of a hill for almost twenty years, the valley was a new experience for the senses. At first she had wondered how these people coped, living at the bottom of a deep bowl. But in a few short weeks she had come to appreciate the grandeur of the steep, wooded hillsides with houses seemingly clinging to the edge, to the sight of sheep grazing high up—the beauty of a different light. Each pathway through the valley had its own attractions—the stately movement of the canal boats, the herons skimming over the river weir, the occasional roaring of the trains along the tree-lined track, and the constant hum from the road traffic. The centre of the town itself felt like a village fair in continuous motion with its numerous coffee and craft shops, markets, cyclists, ramblers, and street performers. The charm of the place was growing on her.

With the disappearance of the sun behind the western hills, Robin started to feel chilled. Time to move. She decided to try the wine bar in the centre of town. Jo had informed her that it was *the* lesbian hangout. Time to see if she could find someone to warm her bed for the night.

†

The drive back to the farm didn't seem to take as long as the drive to the restaurant. Kathryn had suggested they have coffee and a nightcap at Starling Hill. Ellie was in a mellow mood, although Kathryn was sure she had drunk more of the wine during dinner.

Back at the farm Ellie made coffee and brought out the new bottle of brandy. They had finished off the last one celebrating the news of Sophie's pregnancy. Kathryn looked through the CD collection in the living room and finally settled on the combination of Emmylou Harris and Mark Knopfler to set a soothing and, hopefully, romantic tone. She turned on the lamp and switched off the overhead light. Ellie arrived with the drinks and surprised Kathryn by joining her on the couch.

Kathryn poured them each a generous measure of the brandy.

Ellie giggled. "Why, Professor, I do believe you're trying to get me drunk."

"No. It's Dutch courage, for me."

"Am I so scary?"

"At times you are."

"What times are those?"

"Times like this. When I want to kiss you but don't know if you're going to tell me to fuck off."

Ellie picked up both brandy glasses and handed one to Kathryn. She arched an eyebrow. "Here's to Dutch courage, then." Clinking her glass to Kathryn's she took a large gulp and placed the remaining portion back on the table. Kathryn followed her actions, then leant towards her and brushed her lips lightly with her own. Ellie wasn't pushing her away, so she kissed her more fully and felt the response she desired. Placing one hand on the back of Ellie's head she pulled her closer and let her other hand gently explore the nearest breast. The scent of the woman was driving her mad, her clit was demanding attention. Ellie's nipple had hardened under her touch and she knew there was no turning back now, for either of them.

"Could we find somewhere more comfortable?" she murmured in her ear.

*Jen Silver*

"This works for me," Ellie said, sliding a hand down the front of Kathryn's trousers.

Kathryn couldn't control the moan that escaped from her mouth. Ellie's fingers had reached her wetness and she pushed up eagerly to meet the exploring hand.

"Oh God, Ellie. Don't stop." Kathryn knew from their previous sessions how strong Ellie was, the strength in her arms and hands developed over years of moulding clay. "More, please!" Ellie's fingers probed and teased. Letting out a most un-professor-like yell as she came, Kathryn rolled over and fell off the couch.

"Kathryn! Are you okay?" Ellie's face, above hers, was grinning mischievously, as if she didn't know what she had just achieved.

"I'm okay. But you won't be, when I get hold of you."

Ellie's grin widened. She jumped off the couch and headed for the stairs. Kathryn struggled to her feet, shrugged off her trousers and ran after her.

†

It had taken Michelle some time to reach Jo in the pub and then it was another ten minutes before she was able to get her attention. She had to shout to give her Robin's message.

Jo stayed for a few more minutes then excused herself. She didn't know why she felt responsible for Robin. It wasn't dark yet and she wouldn't have known where to start looking but fortunately she spotted Robin walking away from the river. Jo was able to keep her in view as she ambled slowly through the town and when she entered the wine bar Jo debated with herself whether or not to follow. If Robin was looking for a casual shag it was really none of her business.

Her eyes adjusted slowly to the dark interior as she descended the stairs to the basement bar. They had done

102

their best to brighten up the windowless rooms with pictures on the walls, the work of local artists. There weren't many customers, a few people having an early dinner. Robin was standing at the bar and hearing her footsteps on the bare wooden floor turned on her. "Are you following me?"

Jo shrugged. "I saw you come in. These drinks are on me, anyway. I'll have one of those as well." She indicated the bottle on the counter, a pale Belgian beer.

Robin scowled at her but followed her to a table when the two bottles of Leffe were poured out into the round globe-shaped glasses and paid for. "Pretty dead in here."

"It's a bit early if you're looking for action."

"Who says I am?"

"Well, let me think. It's been what, three weeks since you left the farm. And then it was a few weeks before that when you last saw Jasmine. Must be a personal best for you in the celibacy department."

"Seven weeks." Robin chugged back some of her beer.

"Wow. Impressive!"

"Leave it out, Jo. Sarcasm doesn't suit you."

They sipped their drinks in silence. A few more people came in. Robin swirled the remnants of the liquid in the bottom of the round glass. "I'm going to take up boxing."

"Oh. You were talking to Michelle, then."

"Yeah. So, I'm going to go up to the farm tomorrow and collect some more clothes. What time do the diggers arrive?"

"Just after nine, I think. I usually get there after they've started."

A few more people started to arrive. Jo decided against having another beer and left Robin on her own to go and talk to someone else she knew. Considering she had only been in the valley a few months, she hadn't wasted time making friends. For the most part they were customers who liked her crafts or fellow stallholders, others were dog-walkers she met when she was out with Harry. It all added to her decision to put down roots in this place. It felt like home.

†

Robin gunned the bike up the track. It was only after eight but she wanted to make sure she was out of there before the busload of students arrived for the day's dig.

Parking outside the house, she realised what was wrong with the picture. The professor's sporty red car was parked at a rakish angle by the front door. And at that moment, the professor herself came out of the farmhouse door, a big smile on her face as she breathed in the fresh early morning air. The smile faded rapidly when she saw Robin.

"What are you doing here?"

"Just collecting some things." Robin glared at her. "Didn't take you long? Must have missed that class, Seduction 101, is it?"

"Not the only class you missed, it seems. Although you obviously were top of your class in Advanced Cheating on your Partner."

Robin snorted. She was never going to win a contest of words with the professor. She pushed past her and went into the house. No sign of Ellie. Probably still in bed. She rushed upstairs into Aiden's room. With as much haste as possible, she shoved what she needed into her rucksack. Stumbling back downstairs she decided to stop by the living room and collect some of her CDs. The scene that met her eyes rocked her back again. The chinos lying on the floor by the couch were definitely not Ellie's, but the hastily discarded blouse was. Ellie came into the room then.

Robin was torn by conflicting emotions of desire and anger. "Didn't waste any time, did you?"

"Robin, I…"

"Don't bother. I hope you'll be happy together." Unable to stop the tears that were now flowing, Robin pushed past her and made a quick getaway. She stopped the bike when she came to a lay-by. Alone on the deserted road she gave vent to her grief. The sight of Ellie, sleep-tousled, and no doubt replete from a night of lovemaking with the professor, had been a sharp reminder of what she'd so carelessly thrown away. She knew she only had herself to blame, but that didn't make it any easier to accept the situation.

Getting off the bike she leant against the uneven surface of the stone wall and gazed out over the patchwork of farmland spread across the hills. The brown contours of Saddleworth Moor were visible in the distance; fluffy clouds gently moving across the powder blue sky completed the scene. As always the view calmed her. From her vantage point she could just see the top of the church spire in the nearest village.

A large vehicle was lumbering up the hill towards her. It was the coach bringing the university students to Starling Hill for their day's work in the trenches. She waited for it to pass before getting back on her bike and starting her journey back to the Calder Valley.

The conversation she'd had with Jo before leaving that morning came back to her. Jo had been surprised to see her up so early. "I thought you'd pulled last night. When I left you were well into RoRo."

"RoRo?" Robin only had a vague memory of a woman sitting on her lap, stroking her hair.

"Rosie Heywood. Known locally as RoRo—Roll On, Roll Off."

"Jeez. Good thing I took a rain check then."

"Guess there's hope for you, yet."

Hope had just died, she thought glumly. She might as well have given in to RoRo's advances and taken her to bed. Knowing it was Jo's day on the market she had a choice—

moping around the house or helping out on the stall. She decided on the latter. Jo was the only friend she could count on and keeping her sweet was the best option right now.

✝

Ellie collapsed into her chair and curled up into a ball. She hated herself. There was no way she had drunk too much the night before to not be aware of what she had been doing. She had used Kathryn to satisfy her own needs, but it was Robin she had been seeing as their lips met, as their bodies writhed, and fingers probed. It was the release of months of frustration. And now she wished she could turn the clock back. She had seen the flash of desire in Robin's eyes before she stormed out.

After a time she calmed herself, breathing in and out slowly, as taught in the yoga classes she had attended years ago. Moving slowly, mechanically, she cleared away the brandy glasses and coffee mugs. The brandy had been drunk, but the coffee was untouched with now congealing milk on the surface.

She made a fresh pot of coffee and sat down at the kitchen table, feeling the emptiness descend again. Head in hands, she didn't hear the approach of another person until they were touching her shoulder.

"Eleanor?"

Startled, she looked up to find Ed McLaughlin looking down at her, concerned.

"Hi. What is it? Would you like some coffee? It's fresh."

"Um, no. Look, I'm sorry. This doesn't seem like a good time, but I thought maybe you could help."

"Of course. If I can."

He looked towards the door and Ellie realised there was someone else there. Ed called over, "Come on in, Tina. I think you've met before."

106

Ellie recognised the girl as she came into the room. They had talked on the field a few times. She was one of the group she'd originally had trouble identifying as male or female. The dark hair fell over her face, long at the front, but shaved at the back. Each ear had several piercings with a recent one at the edge of one eyebrow. The sleeveless top she wore revealed tattoos on each shoulder and a larger one down her left arm. But it was the dark circles under her eyes that made her look worse than Ellie felt.

"Hi, Tina."

"Tina just needs someone to talk to." Ed started to walk away, obviously relieved to have passed his problem on. "I'll catch up with you later."

Ellie waited until he'd disappeared before saying as calmly as she could, "Have a seat, Tina. Would you like some coffee?"

The girl nodded and moved towards the table.

"Milk and sugar?"

Another nod.

Ellie refilled her own mug and sat down again. "So, what do you want to talk about?"

It took a few sips of coffee before the girl started to talk and then it just tumbled out in a mixture of words and emotions. Ellie quickly got the gist. Tina's parents hadn't been happy with her lifestyle for some time—the hair, piercings, tattoos. But the final straw was when her mother found some books and magazines hidden in her room and discovered their daughter was gay. They couldn't even use the word lesbian.

Finding herself on the street at two in the morning after a prolonged shouting match with her parents, she didn't know where to go. There was no one she could call on at that time. She didn't have any close friends at uni, and the mates she'd had in high school were away at universities further afield. She had eventually found a shelter in the park and stayed there until it got light. Then she'd gone to an early opening café and waited until it was time to get the coach to Starling Hill.

"Do you have a change of clothes with you?" asked Ellie.

"Yes. I managed to grab a few things."

"Okay. Well, I suggest you have a shower and get changed. Then we'll have breakfast. It'll give me time to think about what you can do." She took her upstairs and showed her the bathroom, fetching a towel from the airing cupboard on the way.

Half an hour later, having fed them both scrambled eggs and toast, Ellie led the way into the living room and told Tina to turn on the computer. She had switched the Wi-Fi router on earlier while the girl was in the shower.

"You'll be better at this than me," she said to her, pulling up another chair. "We'll take a look at the university's website first. They should have an LGBT society. Have you never looked them up?"

"No. I didn't think of that."

They found some information on the site, but it was summer holiday time. There wouldn't be anyone around. The new term didn't get underway for another five or six weeks.

Ellie knew she couldn't turn the girl out on the street. "Look, I have a spare room. You can stay here tonight anyway. I'll have a think about what to do next."

Tina gave her a small smile, the first one she'd managed. "Are you sure? I don't want to be any trouble."

"I wouldn't offer if I didn't mean it. Now, do you feel up to getting back to work? I don't want Dr Moss on my case for keeping you away from the trenches."

Tina smiled openly then. "Yes. Absolutely. And thank you so much."

After the girl had gone, Ellie sat back and wondered what she had done. It wasn't like she had much experience with handling teenagers. Tina, despite her external persona, seemed more immature than others her age. But it gave her something else to think about instead of beating herself up about her own problems.

†

Sunlight drifted in through the open doorway. Kathryn stood and watched Ellie as she moved about the studio. All day she had been assaulted by images of Ellie's body, tortured by the remembrance of kissing her soft breasts, the delight of teasing the nipples to a peak of hardness, before moving down to the delicious flavour of sweet juices between her legs.

Ellie finally became aware of her presence and walked slowly towards her. Kathryn bit her lip. There were times when Ellie definitely scared her. It was hard to read her moods. "What's going on? Ed says you've agreed to let Tina Morris stay here."

"Yes." Ellie wiped her hands on the towel she always had hanging from her belt.

"Why?" Try as she could, Kathryn knew she was sounding like a petulant teenager herself.

"She hasn't got anywhere else to go."

"I see. And, what about us?"

"What about us? There is no us, Kathryn. I was a bit tipsy last night. I'm sorry."

Kathryn stared at her, speechless. What had happened in the few short hours since she'd left her bed? Finding her voice at last, she only managed to croak out, "Ellie, I thought last night meant something to you. It did to me."

"I know. Like I said, I'm sorry. It shouldn't have happened."

Kathryn wanted to shake her. "This isn't still about Robin, is it?" Damn the woman. Why did she have to turn up this morning, of all days? Ellie had been so loving last night and she hadn't drunk that much. "You can't keep making excuses for her. She's used you, for years. It's time to move on. You and I, we're good together. You must feel that."

Ellie wasn't looking at her. She was standing still, shoulders slumped, twisting the towel in her hands, staring at the floor. "It's no good, Kathryn. I can't stop thinking about her. Even when I'm with you."

"You're unbelievable!" Kathryn was shaking now. "What was this? Some sort of revenge fuck just to even things up with that bitch? I thought better of you, Ellie." She started to walk away, then turned back at the doorway. "I won't be here tomorrow or Friday. I'm going to London to get feedback on the artefacts I sent to be checked out by experts at the British Museum. See you, Monday. Hopefully, you'll have come to your senses by then."

Kathryn sat in her car, knowing she shouldn't drive off in her current state of mind. In her rearview mirror she saw the girl, Tina, sitting on the step in front of the farmhouse door, the large ginger cat on her lap. She and the cat looked content. Wishing she could feel the same, she turned the key in the ignition. Sometimes having the last word wasn't all that satisfying. She wanted to go back to the studio, take Ellie in her arms, feel her warm breath on her neck. She wanted to go back in time to the night before. But that wasn't possible. She took a deep breath. She was a professional; she had a job to do. And a phone call to make, one she had been putting off out of a sense of loyalty. A loyalty that had just been shattered.

# Chapter Six

## Revelations

The activity in the field looked as busy as ever. Having spent a large part of the day before dealing with an emotional and distressed Robin, Jo hadn't been sure what she would find at the farm.

The news that Kathryn and Ellie had slept together on Tuesday night was hardly a revelation. She had thought it would only be a matter of time. When Robin turned up at the stall on Wednesday morning, one look at her face told the story and her moods during the morning veered between despair and anger. At one point Jo had to tell her she wasn't helping business; potential customers were giving her stall a wide berth. At lunchtime she sent her off to take Harry for a walk. When they returned a few hours later, Robin seemed calmer, but had obviously spent some time in a pub. Her breath reeked of ale.

"I hope you haven't been feeding him rubbish," she said as Harry settled down at her feet contentedly, head between his paws. Robin was a sucker for Harry's pleading brown eyes at the dinner table. And when they ate out, it was Robin's hamburger or meat-filled sandwich he would salivate over.

"Of course not. Only the best for my mate, Harry. A pint of cider and a bowl of chips."

"For God's sake, Robin. Getting rat-arsed in the middle of the day isn't going to solve anything."

"No, but it dulls the pain."

The wet weather wasn't helping business either. So they packed up the stall early. The rest of the day and evening Jo had listened to Robin's tale of woe—how Ellie was the only one for her and how badly she had screwed it up.

The day was starting off overcast, but looked like it was clearing now and going to turn into another fine summer's day, a welcome change from the drizzle of the day before. Jo took a deep breath and went into the house. Ellie was in the kitchen and there were signs that it had been breakfast for two. So, Robin's worst fears were confirmed.

"Hey, is there any coffee left?"

Ellie turned around then and, to her dismay, Jo saw she was crying. Without even thinking about it, she went over and gave her a hug. Ellie collapsed against her and sobbed freely.

Having spent the previous day comforting Robin, Jo was uncomfortable finding herself in the same situation with Ellie. But there wasn't much she could do about it. When Ellie had cried herself out, Jo gently moved her to a seat at the table. She poured them both mugs of coffee.

"What's brought this on?"

"I did something stupid."

"So? Welcome to the club."

"No, I mean really stupid. And I've hurt two people in the process. Three, including myself."

Jo considered this, studying Ellie's face for more clues. All she could see was a woman in torment.

"You seemed okay on Tuesday when I left. So, what happened?"

"Kathryn took me out to dinner. I drank too much." She sniffed and dabbed at her wet eyes. "Robin turned up yesterday morning and I realised I wanted her to stay. But now she thinks Kathryn and I are involved. And I told Kathryn it didn't mean anything, so now she hates me as well."

"Okay. I guess that makes sense, sort of. I mean, Kathryn really fancies you. I thought you two would be good together."

"That's exactly what she said."

"Anyway, Robin doesn't hate you. She's busy hating herself at the moment."

Ellie's head snapped up. "You've seen her."

Jo couldn't meet her eyes. "Well, yes. We're living together. Not like that. Honestly, we're just house-sitting for two friends of mine. We have separate rooms. It's a big house." Jo stopped talking when she realized she was only digging a deeper hole. Ellie's expression had changed dramatically.

"Why didn't you tell me? All this time I've been worried sick about where she was."

"I didn't think it was up to me to interfere. You had kicked her out, after all."

"How long…have you been living together? Can you, at least, tell me that?" Ellie had switched from sad to angry in a moment.

"She turned up about two weeks after she left here. Said she'd stayed with some mates in Leeds for a few days, and then tried Aiden but he turned her down. The house-sitting job was starting the next day and I thought it would be good to have someone else there as it is a big house and even though I've got Harry, he's not much of a guard dog really. I'm sorry I didn't tell you, Ellie, but I'm in the middle here and I don't want either of you to be hurt."

"You say you're not sleeping together. You did have sex with her before, though. So, why not now? It's what she usually does when she's upset."

"It was a one off, Ellie. And she doesn't want me, she wants you."

"She has a funny way of showing it!"

"Well, she knows she's messed up. She's really hurting."

"And I'm not?"

Jo decided to change tack. "Is Kathryn still here?"

"She left yesterday."

"Well, it looks like you had company this morning?" Jo indicated the breakfast remains.

"Oh. Yeah. One of the students is staying here. She's having problems at home." Ellie stood and started clearing up.

"I can do that if you want to get the studio ready."

"Thanks, Jo." Ellie didn't turn around from the sink. "I know I agreed to work with you today, but I think I need to be on my own right now."

It was a dismissal. Jo shook her head. She wished she had been able to lie to Ellie and tell her she hadn't seen Robin. Now, she wasn't sure Ellie would want her around again. As Robin had succinctly put it when she arrived back from the farm yesterday morning, "Everything's gone to shit."

†

Jasmine raced around the flat, tidying up. She had hardly slept since the professor's phone call the evening before. She was sure this was going to be big. It could be Sutton Hoo all over again. Her journalist friend was as excited as she was. They had already drafted the article and found library photos to use plus one of the aerial shots she had taken from Starling Hill. Now they would be able to publish with authentic wording from the site's discoverer.

Kathryn had agreed to meet them at Jasmine's flat. She seemed nervous about meeting in a public place and on the phone she had sounded a bit distraught. Well, they would do their best to put her at her ease. With a selection of sweet and savoury snacks from the Turkish deli down the road, Jasmine carefully set out her best china for tea.

Denise arrived first looking harried. But Jas had never seen her look otherwise. She was always on the move, living on the edge.

"So, where is she?"

"Sorry, Den. I can't move mountains or British Rail. She'll be here in about ten minutes, assuming the train is on time and she can grab a taxi right away. So, chill. Have a pastry. I'm making tea."

"Offer her a proper drink, Jas. Shit, if I'd travelled down from Leeds today, I'd want more than a cup of sodding tea." Denise flopped down on the sofa and draped one of her long jean-clad legs over the arm.

"Behave, will you? This story could be the big one, for both of us."

"So, what's she like? Is she hot?"

"Fuck's sake, Den. This is work. I take it you didn't get laid last night."

"Not for lack of trying. All the women I meet are either married with three kids, or they're total fuck-ups and want to move in with you if you buy them a drink and snatch a snog in the toilets. Anyway, what happened to that love of your life? Wasn't she from some godforsaken place up north as well?"

"She's history."

The polite knock on the door stopped whatever smart remark Denise was going to fire back at her. Jas smoothed down her skirt, not sure why she was feeling nervous.

"Hi, Kathryn. Come in, please." Jas smiled at her visitor, taking in the trim figure dressed in country casuals, crease-free beige cargo pants and mint-green polo shirt. She gestured towards the reclining form on the sofa. "This is Denise Sullivan. She's the writer."

Denise jumped up and shook hands with Kathryn. "Dr Moss. Pleased to meet you."

"Would you like tea or coffee, or something stronger?"

"Something stronger, I think. I'd forgotten how abysmal train travel can be. In the winter there's no heating. In the summer they've got it working and can't turn it off. It was boiling."

Jasmine ignored Den's smirk. "So, what will it be? Beer, wine, G&T?"

"Oh, a gin and tonic would be lovely. Thank you."

"Coming right up." From the kitchen Jas could hear Den's voice, turning on the charm for the professor. They had known each other since high school, running the school magazine between them. Since then their professional lives hadn't crossed, but socially they met up several times a month. Sometimes it was just a quick lunchtime catch-up. But when their schedules meshed they would hit the town together. Until she met Robin, Jasmine hadn't thought she would ever want to settle down with one woman and she knew Den was the same. Their lunchtime sessions were often just a chance to download the crap dates they had both experienced since the last time they went out.

When she appeared in the living room with the tray of drinks—G&T for Kathryn, whisky on the rocks for Den and a bottle of Corona for herself—Denise was sitting next to the professor on the sofa talking animatedly. She stopped when Jas put the tray down on the table.

"I was just telling Kathryn that we have a draft ready and today's chat is informal. We'll just pick out a few quotes to pad out the article."

"Can I see it before you publish?"

"Yes, of course." Den jumped up and rummaged in the shoulder bag she had left by the door, returning moments later with a laptop.

Kathryn sipped at her drink and smiled at Jasmine. "That's wonderful. I'm starting to feel more human already."

"What are your plans for tomorrow?" Jas asked.

"I have a meeting at the British Museum. I sent some artefacts down by courier last weekend. Two top experts are examining them."

"So, the site's definitely Roman."

"Oh, there's no doubt of that. The only questions we have to answer are the who and the why. There was a fort only a few miles away at a place called Slack. It's now mostly covered over by a golf course. So, why was Starling Hill used as a burial site?"

Jasmine looked over at Den and saw she had deftly set up her recorder as well as opening her laptop. "Are there any buildings there? The aerial photos…" she stopped, realising she wasn't meant to know about the photos.

Kathryn gave her a small smile. "It's okay. I know you've got them. Ellie only realised they were missing when we heard the press had got hold of the story."

"Oh, right. But it would be fair to say it was the photos that put you onto the possibility of something there."

"Yes. I had noticed the brickwork in the stables included recognizable Roman cut stones with lime mortar still clinging to them. I also took soil samples on a previous visit to the farm. The results prompted me to fund the aerial survey myself. It might have turned out to be nothing more than builder's rubble or robbed out trenches, but the outlines are clear. We've uncovered several sections of wall, unmistakably Roman construction."

Den chipped in then. "You said you have to find out who was buried there. The artefacts, do they indicate high status?"

"I wouldn't like to comment on that at this stage."

"Okay. But I don't think you would be making this effort for a few bits of pottery. Must be something big and shiny."

Kathryn laughed. "No comment."

"All right. We'll leave that, for now. Tell us about the dig. You're using student labour, I understand."

"Yes, but I would prefer it if you referred to it as fieldwork. They are gaining valuable onsite experience."

They talked for another hour and as Kathryn relaxed, she told them more than perhaps she would have if she hadn't been overwrought from Ellie's abrupt dismissal and the long, hot train journey. Jasmine kept filling up her glass and at the end of the session, she gratefully accepted Den's offer to take her to her hotel.

†

Tina was entertaining Soames, who was in a playful mood; even at four years old he had his kittenish moments. Ellie watched from her chair. The day had been miserable. After the morning's conversation with Jo she had sent her away, unable to cope with having her around. She knew she was being irrational and it wasn't fair to Jo. All the pots she had fired cracked. And it was all down to her impatience and inability to focus on the simplest routines.

Eventually, giving in, she drove down to the village and bought some groceries. Tina had been content with the simple evening meal of baked potato, tinned tuna, and salad. And now she couldn't even concentrate on the book she was trying to read. She put it down and rubbed her eyes.

Tina spoke then. "Um, Miss Winters. Can I ask you something?"

"Sure, but call me Ellie, please."

"Okay."

"What did you want to ask?"

"That boy in the photo on the desk, he's your son?"

"Yes."

"Were you married?"

"Yes. Briefly." She looked across at the girl. Soames had wandered off and she was now picking at the threads on the cushion. "Well, long enough to have Aiden. I left when he was five."

"Why did you leave?"

"I met someone else. A woman. I fell in love."

"Wow! That's amazing."

Ellie supposed it would seem amazing to Tina, who no doubt regarded her as a grandmother who couldn't possibly have had a sex life.

"How did you meet?" the girl asked, not willing to let go of what looked like the beginning of an interesting story.

"She was a nurse. I had taken Aiden for some shots. I guess it was against the rules, but she must have got my home phone number from the patient records." Ellie recalled it clearly. The phone call out of the blue. The woman on the other end hesitatingly saying she wanted to meet her for coffee. And for some reason, she had said she would meet her. Maybe, because she was bored. Gerry was away a lot. Her teaching job was part time but she was planning to go back to it full-time once Aiden started primary school.

"Her name was Susan. At first we did just meet for coffee. Then for lunch on my days off. As things progressed, lunch became a euphemism for three hours in bed at her place. It had been going on for six months before Gerry, my husband, questioned why our son was spending all week at the child-minder's rather than just my three teaching days. I told him I was doing private tutoring."

"Did he find out?" Tina looked the most animated she had seen her since her arrival.

"Yes. We got careless. One Friday evening he came back from a conference early. I wasn't expecting him to be home until the next day. He found us in bed together."

"What happened?"

"He threw me out. Just like your parents did."

"But, what about your son?"

119

"He kept him. Told me I wasn't fit to be a mother. I didn't fight for custody. It was a different time. I was afraid of losing my job."

"So, what happened with you and Susan? Did you stay together?"

"It lasted for about a year. I was trying to get access to Aiden but Susan didn't really want to have a kid around. We started arguing. So, I moved back here to live with my parents, and I got a full-time job in the local high school."

Tina was looking at her, eyes filled with tears. "You lost everything. For love."

"Yes. Sounds romantic, but believe me, it was anything but."

Tina was silent for a few minutes but Ellie sensed she was going to ask her something else. "There's a woman in that picture in the bedroom. Is that Susan?"

Ellie knew the photo she meant. Aiden had taken it when he and Robin were at a music festival. It was an old photo; he must have been seventeen or eighteen at the time. "No. That's Robin. She lived here until recently."

The girl considered this for a moment, then asked, "Don't you get lonely, living out here on your own?"

"Sometimes. Look, Tina, I'm a bit tired. I'm going to turn in early. Watch TV or listen to music if you want, as long it's not too loud. I'll see you in the morning." With that, Ellie stood up and retreated to her bedroom. Collapsing on the bed, she felt the tears start again. Talking about Susan had been a mistake. The pain of that time came back to her. She had loved Susan with all her heart, and for the first time in her life, felt loved in return. Marrying Gerry straight out of school had been a mistake and if she had listened to her parents she would never have done it. But at eighteen she thought she knew better. She was the envy of her peers, having attracted the attention of a handsome, older man. The big car, the four-bedroom detached house in a fashionable suburb of Manchester, had easily lured her. Once they were married it hadn't taken her long to realise that for all his external charm, all he wanted was a trophy wife. He didn't stop her carrying on with her education and getting a history degree. But to him it was just a hobby, something to keep the wife occupied while he was away on business trips. And when Aiden was born, it was like mission accomplished. She hardly existed in his view. Ellie was certain he had affairs but when she strayed he couldn't bear the thought of being cuckolded by a woman.

At first, Ellie had thought Gerry wouldn't want to be burdened with the responsibilities of looking after a five-year-old. She thought it wouldn't be long before he would be happy to give up full custody. But she'd underestimated his need for a nuclear family. He soon had wife number three lined up. It was years later before she realised he had dumped wife number one because she was infertile. He had wanted a son, someone to carry on the name, follow in his footsteps. And it was only recently that she realised if she had stood up to him, he would likely have settled the matter out of court. She had let her own fears take over. His fear, she now knew, would have been to become the laughing stock of his associates. If she'd slept with a man, it wouldn't have been so bad. But your wife leaving you for another woman…that would have been social suicide in his world.

Too many ifs and buts. None of it mattered now. She needed to think about Tina. The girl needed somewhere to stay, and she wasn't going to want to be stuck on the farm for much longer.

†

There was smoke coming out of the kiln's chimney. That was a good sign, Jo thought as she parked her van near the studio. It had taken much soul-searching to help her decide she had to come back and try talking to Ellie. She didn't like leaving it as they had. Robin hadn't been communicative the previous day. She seemed to have talked herself out and spent the evening lying on her bedroom floor listening to music through her headphones. Not sure what to do, Jo had opted to do nothing. She didn't tell Robin that it looked like Kathryn and Ellie were not an item and that Ellie wanted her back.

Walking into the studio, she called out, "Hi, Ellie." To her surprise, the person looking into the kiln was a man she'd never seen before. "Oh, sorry. Is Ellie here?"

He straightened up and looked her up and down. Then he smiled. "You must be Jo. I'm Kieran."

"Um, yes. How did you know?"

"Process of elimination. I've met the other women in Ellie's life. She told me about you wanting to learn how to throw. How's it going?"

Jo decided she liked his smile. "Okay, I guess. Although the bowl I tried to make on Tuesday turned into a misshapen vase. And that's probably putting it politely."

"Well, if you can wait a few moments, I need to make sure the temperature's right for these babies, then we can go over to the house together. Ellie's cooking breakfast. I'm sure she won't mind one more."

"I don't know. We sort of had a disagreement yesterday."

"Well, if I know Ellie, it won't last long. She doesn't bear grudges."

They walked over to the house together. Jo glanced over at the field. "Is the professor not back, then?"

"No. I gather she's in London. Looks like Dr Ed's in charge today. They're bringing in some more eggheads next week."

"Eggheads?"

"Sorry. My disrespectful term for experts. I mean, Ed's okay. But most of the academics I've met are fairly socially challenged."

Kieran called out as they entered the house, "Hey, Ellie. Stick another egg in the pan."

Ellie was standing at the stove when they arrived in the kitchen. She smiled when she saw them. Jo was relieved. It looked like she was forgiven.

"I found this in the studio. Hope you don't mind," Kieran said as he pulled out a chair and sat down.

"Not at all. We have some things to talk about."

"Great. Can you do it after we eat? I'm starving."

"Oh right. Is your cooker broken?"

Jo realised it was just friendly banter. "Can I do anything?"

"Sure. Just help yourself to coffee. And get one for this lazy git as well."

Breakfast was delicious. Jo thought she could never eat anything other than freshly laid farm eggs ever again. Kieran went back to the studio to check on his babies, leaving them to clear up. He had offered to help, but Ellie shooed him out. As soon as they were sitting down with a second mug of coffee, Ellie said, "I want to apologise about yesterday. It's been an emotional few days, but I shouldn't have taken it out on you."

"Well, I felt bad too. That's why I came back today."

"I'm glad you did. You see, I've been thinking about Tina's situation."

"That's the girl who's staying here?"

"Yes. I know it's a major thing to ask, but how would you feel about giving her a place to stay? You said this house was big."

Jo looked at her. "I think I'd like to meet her before I can agree to that. It's not my house."

"Of course. The thing is, I think, it would probably do her good to get away from here for a while. She'll be going back to uni at the start of term. But I thought maybe she could get a job, meet some other people."

"What is her problem, exactly?"

Ellie explained how Tina's parents had reacted to finding out she was gay. "I don't think she's ever had a relationship. For all her macho appearance, she's actually very shy. So, what do you think?"

"Well, there aren't a lot of jobs around. But if she doesn't mind bar work or waitressing, she might just find an opening. There are a lot of cafés and bars in HB. Or, if she likes this sort of thing, she might be able to do gardening. Does she want to stop working here?"

"I haven't asked her. I thought I better sound you out first."

"And wouldn't you have to check with the professor? She'll be losing one of her workers."

"All right. It was just an idea. You're obviously not keen."

"No, I didn't say that. I would just like to think about it."

"Look, you could meet her when they have their lunch break. And if you really don't think it's a good idea, I respect that. I'll think of something else."

Jo agreed and went out to the studio with Ellie and was soon immersed in attempting to create another bowl.

†

Kathryn watched the people walking past. She was sitting at an outside table of the restaurant where she had agreed to meet Denise after her consultation at the museum. It was sunny on the south side of the Thames and there was a constant flow of pedestrians enjoying the warmth. It was days like this when Kathryn thought she could adapt to city life.

"Hey, have you ordered drinks?"

Kathryn looked up to see the journalist looking down at her, eyes unreadable behind dark shades.

"Not yet. I thought I'd better wait for you."

Denise placed her bag carefully on the spare chair, beckoning to the waiter as she pulled out the other seat and sat down opposite Kathryn. When he'd taken their order and disappeared, she asked, "How did it go with the boffins?"

"No comment," Kathryn said, smiling.

"Look, it's off the record." Den placed her hands on the table, palms up. "No secret notebook or recordings."

"One thing I've learned. With journalists, it's never off the record."

Their drinks arrived—a white wine spritzer for Kathryn, an Italian lager for Denise—giving Kathryn the opportunity to change the subject. "How long have you known Jasmine?"

"Too long. Best mates in high school."

"Just mates?"

"Now who's fishing for info?" Denise grinned at her and took a large gulp of beer. "Yeah, we tried it once, but it didn't really work. What about you? Jas thinks you and this Ellie are an item."

"It didn't really work either. She's in love with someone else."

"Aha. Let me guess, the roving Robin."

"For someone who's never been north of Watford, you seem to know a lot about life up north."

"I keep my ear to the ground...and my nose in other people's business." She laughed, seeing Kathryn's expression. "Jas has been banging on about Robin for the last six months. I've just been waiting for the call to help her pack the U-Haul. Now, it seems, it's off."

Kathryn grimaced. She really didn't want to think about Robin and her seemingly unbreakable hold over Ellie. "Can we change the subject?"

"Fine. Where would you like to go for dinner?"

"I thought we were eating here?"

"This dump. No way. My rep would be shot."

"I'm happy sitting here and I think the menu looks okay."

"Maybe by Huddersfield standards, but you're in the big city now."

Kathryn gave in and let Denise lead the way. It was, she decided, nice to let someone else take charge for a change. She had a pretty clear idea what Den's motives were. Not just to get her to talk about the dig, but to get her into bed. The attraction had been immediate from the day before when they met in Jas's flat. It surprised her—she didn't normally go for the tall, masculine-looking types—but there was something about Den's smile and the sparkle in her eyes. She seemed to be aiming for a street-surfer look with her short, but stylishly cut, dirty blonde hair and attire consisting of sleeveless grey T-shirt and well-worn, low-slung jeans.

When she saw the prices on the menu of the restaurant Den finally pronounced as suitable, Kathryn said she would pay her way. Den just gave her a mischievous grin and said, "Yeah. You will."

They were well into the main course before Den attacked with a throw-away comment. "You know, I think there are similarities to the findings in Cirencester two years ago. What was it they found? Over forty skeletons. And the one in Norfolk was even bigger. Not a lot of bling found so they figured they were Christian burials. Are yours Christians, do you think?"

"Nice try, Sherlock. My prawns are delicious. How's the pigeon?"

"Duck, Professor."

"Doctor professor to you."

Den raised her eyebrows flirtatiously. "So what's a nice professor doctor like you doing in a place like Huddersfield?"

"It's lovely there, actually. The town's built on seven hills, like Rome."

"Every town north of Watford makes that claim."

"You know," Kathryn gave Den a wide smile, "there is something you can add to your article."

"What's that, o wise one."

"Stop taking the piss and I might tell you."

Den sat back, eyes wide, all innocence.

"We can't rule out a connection with the Brigantes. West Yorkshire was the hub of their operations. And thanks to their leader at that time, Queen Cartimandua, the tribe had strong links with the Romans."

"Is that it?"

"That's all I can tell you, for now."

"You are such a tease, Professor. Fancy dessert?"

"Now who's teasing?"

"Your place or mine?"

"I'm guessing mine's closer."

Without needing to say anything else, Den signalled to the waiter to bring the bill. And without arguing, Kathryn let her pay. They made it to her hotel room with all their clothes on, just. As soon as the door closed, Den's hands reached around Kathryn's body and unclasped her bra. She pulled her close and they kissed. For the second time that week, Kathryn found herself in a heightened state of desire. She moaned softly as Den caressed her left breast and started to explore her mouth with her tongue. Den had also forced one of her legs between hers, which she gripped tightly and rode with increasing urgency. Den's other hand grasped her buttock and she was on the verge of coming in the most undignified way she could remember since one of her earliest sexual encounters.

Sex with Den was rougher than she was used to, but she enjoyed it. Waking up in the middle of the night, lying in a wet patch in the bed, she found herself grinning inanely. She'd known this woman less than thirty-six hours and already felt as if they had known each other forever. Falling in love with someone like Denise Sullivan probably wasn't a good idea. She didn't look like the marrying kind. But it could be fun for a while. And, for a few hours anyway, the heartbreak she had left behind at Starling Hill had receded to a distant speck on the horizon.

She slept soundly for the rest of the night and didn't hear Den leave. When she woke again, sunlight was streaming through the light hotel curtains. In the dawning of a new day she was overcome by a sense of guilt. Why had she given in so readily to the reporter's advances? A strand of her hair glinted on the pillow next to her. She twisted it in her hands, wishing it was a golden strand of Ellie's and that she could have woken up beside her.

✝

Pushing open the heavy door, the smell of sweat and unwashed bodies assaulted her nostrils. Robin carried on and walked into the training area. A number of large, heavy-looking punch bags were dangling from hooks around the room. A full-sized boxing ring took up one corner. And the length of one wall held a collection of weights, gloves, and pads.

Michelle spotted her and came over. "Hey, you made it. Great. Look, the first session's free, but I just need you to fill out this form. Make sure you're not going to keel over on us."

"Okay. Thanks."

After answering the health-related questions on the form, Robin found a place against a wall to put her bag. She hadn't known what to bring, but Jo thought she should take a small towel and a bottle of water. It was a warm day so she had just worn shorts and a T-shirt. Others started to drift in. Michelle introduced her. There were half a dozen and she knew she wasn't going to remember who was who. They started off doing warm-up exercises and Robin realised she was going to struggle to keep up. She had never done any kind of organised fitness training. Helping Ellie with the pottery preparation and doing odd jobs around the farm had been all the exercise she'd had since leaving school.

The boxing part was fun but hard work. Michelle kept them at it for the best part of an hour, and then took them through the warm-down exercises. "You okay?" she asked Robin when they'd finished.

Robin nodded, still catching her breath.

"It'll get easier."

"Really?"

"Yeah. These guys have been doing it for a few years now. So you did well for a first time."

"Some of them look pretty fit."

Michelle grinned at her. "And in which sense are you using the word fit?"

"Both, I guess."

"Well, if you came here looking for love, forget it. They're all spoken for, one way or another."

"Story of my life." Robin finished drying off the sweat, gave her hair a final rubdown and shoved the towel into her bag.

"I don't have another class today. Want to go for a drink, and you can tell me about it?"

Robin nodded and followed Michelle out onto the street, waiting while she locked the door. They walked slowly over to the pub where they'd met earlier in the week. It was quieter now. They sat downstairs where the flag-stoned floor helped to keep the place cool in the midday heat. Robin found herself telling Michelle about her dilemma, the realisation, possibly too late, that she had lost the woman she loved. She gave her a slightly abridged version, leaving out the one-night stand with Jo.

"What about you?" she asked, once they were on their second beer and she'd run out words. "Any significant other?"

"Are you hitting on me?"

"I wouldn't dare. You could knock me out with your little finger."

Michelle laughed. "As it happens, I'm married. My wife and I have been together for ten years. We have two kids."

"Wow! You must think I'm a real arse then."

"Depends."

"On what?"

"On what you do now. If you want her back it seems to me you need to be proactive."

"How can I even compete? The professor is everything I'm not. She's clever, has a good job, and doesn't sleep around. And right now she's at the farm every day."

"Sounds too good to be true. No one's that perfect. There'll be a flaw somewhere."

They talked for a bit longer, and then Michelle said she had to go. Robin retrieved her bike from the nearby car park and rode back to the house. The morning's exercise and chat with Michelle had energised her. She took her laptop out into the garden with a glass of water and reviewed the works in progress. The truth was she had hardly made a start on either of them. But with a clearer head she could see what needed doing and with a little application on her part she thought she could knock them into shape over the weekend.

Harry nudging her knee with his nose brought her back into the real world. He had soon settled down when she had first come outside with him and had been sleeping in the shade while she worked.

"Okay, bud. What time is it?" The clock on her laptop showed 5:28. "Oh, I guess you're hungry, then. Wonder what's keeping Jo." The coolness of the early evening should have alerted her to the time but she had been engrossed in setting up the navigation on one of the sites and making sure all the links worked.

Closing the laptop, she went into the kitchen followed by an eager dog. After giving Harry his evening portion of food, she checked to see what was in stock for dinner. It looked like it was going to be pasta again. If she wanted any high-energy protein she would have to eat some of Harry's dog food.

The sound of Jo's camper van rattling into the track relieved her of having to make that decision. Robin was sure she could talk her into getting another takeaway. Jo arrived in the kitchen, breathless and clutching another pot. This one looked like it might pass as a bowl. Another person of indeterminate sex followed her into the house.

"Robin, this is Tina. She's going to be staying with us for a few days, anyway. What do you think? Isn't this the greatest?" She held out the lumpy object for Robin's inspection.

"Um, yeah. It's good, Jo. It actually looks like a bowl. Hi, Tina." Robin held her hand out towards the youngster, who she could now see was definitely a girl.

"I'll show Tina to her room. What about a takeaway? I've heard the Thai's quite good. There's a menu in that drawer by the fridge."

"Okay. Do you want me to order for you?"

"Yeah. Just get a selection of dishes we can share."

"Are you a veggie, Tina?"

"No." The girl still hadn't looked directly at her. She seemed to be hiding behind her fringe.

"Good. I can order some real food for us to share."
Robin started dialling the Thai restaurant's number as Jo led
Tina upstairs.

Jo came back into the kitchen a few minutes later with a
bundle of clothes. "These need washing. They're all Tina has
and she's been wearing them for the last few days. She's
taking a shower now. Hope you don't mind, I've lent her one
of your T-shirts and a pair of shorts."

"Okay. What's happened to her?"

"Her parents threw her out when they found out she's a
lesbian."

"I would have thrown her out for having a Mallory Knox
tattoo. She's going to regret that before she's much older."

"She's a bit shy, so go easy on her, please."

The Thai food and a few beers helped to relax the
teenager although she only spoke if asked a question. Robin
managed to find out that she was only part of the dig because
she had attended one of Dr Moss's lectures and thought that
archaeology sounded exciting. However, taking part in the
excavation at Starling Hill had made her realise that the
actual fieldwork was quite boring. She didn't mind the
physical labour but the day-to-day trench work could be
mind-numbingly tedious. And she didn't really know any of
the other students.

"You thought Professor Moss was pretty hot, I bet," said
Robin.

Jo shot her a warning look that she ignored.

"She's okay," said Tina, and this time she did look
directly at Robin. "But Miss Winters is really fit."

Robin swallowed. "Yeah. She is. Really fit." She pushed
back from the table. "Look, if you don't mind, I'll leave you
two with the cleaning up. I need to do some work."

✝

"I didn't mean to upset her."

"Maybe not. But I think you knew she was Ellie's partner. She's still hurting." Jo wondered if it had been a good idea to take the youngster on. But when she met her and saw how vulnerable she looked, she had agreed with Ellie's plan. "Well, let's clear this lot away and then I think Harry needs a walk. Do you want to come?"

Jo kept Harry on his lead until they reached the park. There were a lot of people about enjoying the balmy evening sunshine. Groups of kids, younger than Tina, lolled about on the grass in different states of undress and intoxication. The more energetic and less stoned were getting a workout on the skate park, flipping their boards with practiced nonchalance.

Once through the park it was quieter along the canal and Tina started to talk. Jo had asked her if she'd ever had a relationship with a woman. Tina's response, hesitant at first, didn't surprise her. She remembered her own high school days only too well. Tina's best friend was her first major crush but she hadn't said anything, hadn't even come out to her when they were older. Afraid to lose her friendship.

"Where is she now?" Jo asked.

"Hayley? She got in at Durham, studying engineering, of all things."

"Hasn't she come home for the summer?"

"No, she's doing a surveying job, somewhere near Bristol."

"Well, you could still contact her. Maybe send her an email, explain what's happened."

"What if she doesn't want to talk to me when she knows why they threw me out?"

"If she's a true friend, she won't. Sometimes you have to stop worrying about how other people will react. Anyway, you might find she's not too surprised. She might have already sussed you out."

"Yeah. Well, I never really had any boyfriends. I just couldn't pretend to be interested. I mean, there were some guys I hung out with. We'd talk about music, films, and stuff. And I went to the Year 11 Prom with Sam. He was pretty geeky, but even so I think I was last on his list of possible dates."

"And you never talked about boys with Hayley? That would have been a massive clue. She must be pretty bright if she's doing Engineering at Durham. Give her some credit."

The weekend progressed without any further awkwardness. Robin stayed out of the way for most of Saturday and Sunday, immersed in her work. Jo took Tina into the town on Saturday and showed her the variety of cafés and bars she could apply to for jobs. She told her they would approach some of them on Monday when it was less busy. Weekends were the peak time for all the businesses. They spent a lot of time in the CD shop with Tina and the proprietor discussing the merits of various bands Jo had never heard of. Unfortunately he didn't have a job he could offer her, but told her to pop in any time if she wanted a chat.

Sunday turned out to be another scorcher so they spent the morning lounging in the back garden, reading and snoozing in the sun. Harry stayed in the shade of the big chestnut tree.

Robin emerged from the house after lunch and in a playful mood, flicking water onto Jo's bare torso. Jo opened one eye and asked, "You won the lottery?"

"Nope. Finished those two jobs and I've already had a response from one of them. They liked what I've done and have recommended me to someone else."

"Excellent."

"So, you two lazy buggers up for a swim?"

The pool was an indoor one, separate from the house, in a chalet-style wooden building but with sliding glass doors to open out during the warmer months. The boys had plans to add a sauna on to the side when they returned from their Canadian adventures.

"I don't have a swimsuit with me," said Tina.

"You don't need one. There's nobody here but us." Robin grinned at her as she pulled her T-shirt over her head and shrugged out of her shorts. "Last one in's a wimp," she called out, racing towards the pool.

Jo gazed after her, wishing, not for the first time since they had moved in together, that her housemate wasn't still obsessing over Ellie. Robin attracted her and seeing her naked made it difficult to keep to her self-imposed promise not to get involved again. But wishful thinking would get her nowhere. She looked over at Tina who was staring open-mouthed in the direction of the pool. Robin had opened the doors and then executed a perfect dive into the deep end.

"Come on then. We can't let her have all the fun."

"But, I can't..." Tina looked down at her body, obviously embarrassed by the thought of stripping off completely.

"Don't worry. It's nothing we haven't seen before." Taking her by the hand, she led the reluctant youngster towards the pool. After she'd taken off her own clothes and got into the water, Tina slowly and shyly removed her own garments and lowered herself cautiously into the shallow end.

✝

"Jesus, Den. Where did you get this stuff?" Jasmine couldn't believe what she was seeing.

The journalist shrugged, noncommittal.

"Fuck! You slept with her, didn't you? I'm meeting her at the TV studio for this interview in half an hour. How can I look her in the eye?"

"You know nothing."

"I know you. And this is pretty underhanded, even by your low standards."

"Look. She's sitting on a gold mine. It's in the public interest."

"Yeah, right." Jas was exasperated by her friend's blasé attitude. "That's what all those *News of the World* reporters said, and look what happened to them."

"Hey, it's not like I tapped her phone or anything."

"No, you just accessed her photos and emails on her phone while she was asleep. After you fucked her, of course."

"Look, Jas. Don't worry about it. Just go with the flow."

"You are seriously pissing me off, Denise."

"Just go and get her set up for the interview. I'll look after the fallout."

Jasmine shook her head. She was having second thoughts about involving Den in this business, but it was too late now. The article would already be on the presses. Well, as Denise said, she didn't know anything. If the shit hit the fan, she was in the clear. Time to go and meet the professor and make sure some good sound bites came out of the interview.

†

Kathryn sat back in her seat. The train was filling up, but first class was still empty. Two businessmen in suits were at the table further down the aisle. She had her two-seater window table to herself although there was a ticket on top of the seat opposite indicating it was booked. Hopefully, they wouldn't get on until Peterborough.

Waking up on Saturday morning, she had been disappointed to find Den gone. But in a way she was relieved. The morning after could be an embarrassment, wondering what to say. She didn't have a lot of experience with one-night stands, but she had usually been the one who crept away before the reality of the situation set in. No need to make false promises to keep in touch or make plans for another date.

The train started moving and the seat opposite was still empty. She opened the newspaper to look for the article. Jasmine had said it would be in the Focus section of the main part of the paper. Originally they wanted to get it in the magazine but that always went to print earlier in the week. It was a surprise then to see a large image on the front page of one of the artefacts she had been examining with the experts at the museum on Friday. The caption read *Important Celtic find at remote farm in West Yorkshire. Experts have dated the gold torque as first century. See page 5 for the in-depth report.*

Where had they gotten that photo? Frantically, she turned the pages to find page five. It was a full-page article, with the byline, Denise Sullivan. There was a small photo of her, several large photos of another dig site, Cirencester she guessed, plus one of the aerial ones of Starling Hill. She was deep into the text, fascinated by the detail she didn't know she'd provided, when she became aware of someone sitting down.

"Good read, huh?"

She looked up, startled, to see Den grinning at her.

"What are you doing here? That seat's booked."

"Yes. For me. I wanted to come and have a look at the site."

"How did you know...?" Kathryn stared at her. Comprehension dawned. She shook her head. "Never trust a journalist. You're a real piece of work, you are."

"Thanks."

The train was picking up speed, leaving the sprawl of the city suburbs behind. Kathryn could feel her temper rising.

"Did you and your good mate, Jasmine, cook this little scam up between you?"

"Jas knew nothing about it. Look, I know you don't think much of me right now. But we needed that info to complete the story. The thing's gone viral on the Internet already."

Kathryn couldn't keep the hurt out of her voice. "Friday night. Did it mean anything at all to you? Other than another way to screw me?"

"Actually, it did. You might not believe me, but I do really like you Kathryn. You're an amazing woman."

Her phone's ringtone stopped her from replying. The businessman facing her way gave her a hard stare. It was a silent carriage. Ignoring his look, she took the call. The screen image had shown her it was Ed calling. "Yes, I've seen it." Pause. "You can't keep anything secret nowadays. Journalists have their tricks." She glared at Denise over her glasses. "I can't say more now. I'm on the train. Can you just make sure security is in place tonight? Yes, tonight. Thanks. See you later." She got up from her seat. "I have to make another call."

Going out into the corridor, swaying with the train's movement, she called Ellie. No answer. And no answerphone. She was probably in the studio. Knowing that she hardly ever watched television or read newspapers, Kathryn thought it was probably best she remain in ignorance of what was happening. She called Ed back. "I'm onto it, Kathryn," he said irritably.

"Sorry, Ed. I'm sure you are. It's Ellie I'm worried about. She's not answering her phone. Is she on her own? Or is Tina Morris still there?"

"She's on her own, I guess. Tina went off with the hippie woman on Friday to stay with her over the weekend. Eleanor said she would talk to you about it, but she thought Tina should have a change of scene."

"Okay. That's probably sensible. But I'm worried about her being there on her own tonight. And not being able to even contact her to tell her what's happening. She won't have seen the news."

"All right. Look, I'll be going up with the security team. I need to show them around. So, I'll make sure I see her."

"Thanks. And I really am sorry. This has all gotten out of hand."

"That's an understatement." He ended the call abruptly.

Kathryn returned to her seat. The journalist had plugged in her laptop and was staring intently at the screen.

"You have no idea of the shit-storm you've created."

"I think I do. Look." She turned the screen around. "This is your interview on YouTube. Over a thousand hits in the last hour. And, as I said before, it's already trending on Twitter. And my email inbox is full." She smiled at her. "And do you know how sexy you are when you're angry?"

"Don't even go there." Kathryn took a deep breath. Denise had trapped one of her legs under the table. "What are you planning to do when you get to Leeds?"

"I thought I'd go and see Eleanor Winters. Another side of the story."

"No! Ellie's off limits."

"Ooh. Ellie, is it? Something going on there? You're quite the player, Professor."

"Seems to me you're the player. There are plenty of empty seats. I would appreciate it if you would go and sit somewhere else."

Denise gazed at her intently, then shrugged and closed her laptop. Without saying another word she removed herself and her belongings and moved to a seat further down the carriage.

She was now out of Kathryn's line of sight but she was still uncomfortably aware of the journalist's presence. Her rational self seemed to take a nap when Denise was around.

At her age, she shouldn't be reacting like a hormonal teenager to the presence of an attractive younger woman. And someone who had abused her trust so callously at that. She turned her attention back to the newspaper article. But she couldn't read more than a few lines before her eyes blurred with tears. When she had contacted Jasmine on Wednesday evening, her desire to hit back at Ellie had been so strong. And she thought she would be in control, as always. What harm was there in talking to a journalist, doing a television interview? It was only sensible to make sure the facts were presented clearly. Trending on Twitter. She didn't even know what that meant but seeing the excited glow on Den's face she figured it was success in terms of generating publicity. A social media feeding frenzy. And she had unleashed it. Well, it was done now. The only thing she could do was sit tight and ride out the storm. And hope that at some point she would be able to explain what had happened to the one person who really mattered in all this, Ellie.

†

Saturday had been quiet on the farm. Ellie wandered around the dig site, taking in the extent of the excavations. It had taken on a life of its own, growing rapidly over the space of the last two weeks. There was something Kathryn was holding back. The artefacts she'd sent off to the British Museum were high status. Ellie knew that from her own studies. But what did it mean?

Sheep had grazed this field for hundreds of years. Her family had been sheep farmers. When her father died, she'd sold the sheep as neither she nor her mother had either the inclination or physical capabilities to manage the stock. And she had wanted to pursue her interest in pottery.

Over the years she'd had numerous offers for the land. She had resisted, mainly because she loved the landscape and the sense of her heritage, of belonging. But now, she wondered if it wasn't time to let go, to move on. But move on to where, to what? She wished, more than anything that she could talk to Robin about it. Jo hadn't told her where this house was. She'd had a mad thought to drive over to Hebden Bridge and see if she could locate it by finding the camper van. Trawl the local pubs to find someone who knew Jo Bright Flame.

She could just phone Robin. But something stopped her. How could she explain what had happened with Kathryn? Robin thought she was involved in a steamy love affair now.

Sunday morning the phone rang at eight o'clock. She answered, hoping it would be Robin. The person on the other end started by asking if she was Eleanor Winters. It was too early for a telesales call, even for a double-glazing company. After she confirmed who she was, the caller said they wanted to talk to her about the important Roman finds at the archaeological dig on her land. "And who are you?" she asked. When the caller said they were from a national newspaper, she said, "No comment," and put the phone down on them. It immediately rang again. She ignored it. After twenty rings it stopped. Then it started again. She unplugged it from the wall socket.

She went out to the pottery studio and tried to concentrate on creating a bowl, a design she'd been mulling over for some time. But it ended up looking like something Jo would have produced. The line of cracked pots from the failed firing the other day mocked her from their place on the window ledge.

The sound of vehicles arriving in the farmyard roused her from her torpor. It was a relief to see Ed McLaughlin emerge from the first car. Several burly men in uniform emerged from the other one.

"Eleanor." He greeted her warmly. "Remember, we talked about security. These fellows are here to do the job.

I'll just show them what's what, and then I wouldn't mind having a private word with you."

She nodded and smiled at him. "Certainly. I'll put the kettle on. Would these guys like a drink?"

"No. You don't have to wait on them. They have their own supplies."

†

Ed sat across from her and spread out the newspaper. "I'm sorry. This was a shock to me, too. You have to believe me. I didn't know she was going to do this. She's also been on TV. The interview went out early this morning and I understand it's gone out on YouTube as well."

Ellie looked at the photo on the front page of the paper. Slowly, she turned the pages to the article inside. She scanned the words, aware of Ed watching her.

"That's an old picture of Kathryn," she said, not looking up.

"It's the one on the university website. Her PR photo, I guess."

"Have you talked to her today?"

"Yes, she called me from the train. She says she tried to phone you. In her defence, I don't think she expected this level of publicity."

"I had to unplug my phone."

Ed nodded sympathetically. "Is there anyone who could stay with you tonight? I'm not sure you should be out here on your own."

"I've lived here most of my life, Ed. I don't mind being on my own." He didn't seem convinced with this answer, but in the end he accepted her decision and drove off assuring her he would be back first thing in the morning.

Part Three

## Chapter Seven

## Conciliations

The phone was ringing and it wasn't part of the dream. Robin groped around and finally reached the device on the bedside table. The clock showed it was five fifteen. She answered groggily and it took her a moment to realise it was Aiden babbling away on the other end.

"What the fuck, Aid? Do you know what time it is?"

"Rob, it's Sophie. She's in hospital. And I can't reach my mum. Her phone's permanently engaged."

"Okay. Calm down." Robin sat up. "Start at the beginning. Why is Sophie in hospital?"

"She's had some bleeding. I don't know. I'm scared. She might lose the baby."

"Which hospital?"

"Bury."

"Okay. Look, you know how phone-phobic your mum is. Knowing her she'll have taken it off the hook for some reason. I'll go up to the farm and get her. And ring me again when you know anything."

"Right. Thanks, Rob." He sounded about fifteen again.

"And Sophie's in the right place. Just be there for her, whatever happens."

Robin dressed as quickly as she could, left a note for Jo, and rolled the bike down the drive so as not to wake up the household. Praying there were no speed traps out early on a Monday morning, she set out to break all records for the drive to Starling Hill. Slowing down on the final ascent to the farm, she was stunned by the presence of police cars and a roadblock. She stopped by the barrier and removed her helmet. "What's going on?" she asked as the officer approached her.

"No access. Only for residents."

"Well, I live here. Starling Hill farm. I've been away."

"Name."

"Robin Fanshawe."

"Sorry. We've been told there's only an Eleanor Winters at this address."

"Well, if you check the electoral roll you'll find I'm on it. Anyway, this is an emergency. I've had a call from her son. His fiancée's in hospital and I'm picking Ellie up to take her there."

The policeman didn't look like he was buying this. "Look, we've spent most of the night clearing the media circus out of here. I have to admit, though, your story's more original than any I've heard so far."

"It's true. Here," she dug her phone out, "talk to Aiden and ask him." She dialled Aiden's number and handed the phone to the policeman. He walked away from her and spoke into it. Coming back a few minutes later, he handed her the phone. "Okay. Sounds genuine. Off you go. I'll radio ahead to let my colleague know you're coming."

Relieved, Robin drove carefully up the farm track. There was another police officer outside the door. She nodded to Robin and opened the front door for her.

The kitchen light was on and Robin found Ellie sitting at the table with a mug of tea in front of her. She hardly ever drank tea in the morning. "Robin, what are you doing here?"

Robin stood awkwardly in the doorway. "Sophie's been taken into hospital. Aiden said he couldn't get through on the phone."

"Oh God. I had to take if off the hook. The calls were driving me mad."

"Well, whenever you're ready, I said I would take you over to Bury."

"Right. I'll just be a few minutes. The kettle's boiled if you want to make yourself a drink."

A hot drink would take too long so Robin helped herself to orange juice from the fridge. There was no sign of the cats but their food bowls were empty. Not knowing how long they would be she put food out for them and two bowls of water. The cats might have to fend for themselves if Ellie needed to be away overnight so she filled the sink with water as well. Soames wasn't fussy about drinking out of the toilet bowl either.

Ellie appeared then dressed in jeans and a sweatshirt.

"You'll need a jacket. It'll be cold on the bike," Robin told her.

"Can't we take the Jeep?"

"The bike will be quicker." Robin followed her out into the hallway.

Ellie scrabbled through the coats hanging up and found her old leather jacket. "Do they know what's wrong with Sophie?"

"Aiden only said she'd had some bleeding. I don't think he's coping well."

"He wouldn't. He's a total wimp when it comes to the sight of blood."

Once outside, Robin got the spare helmet out while Ellie spoke to the policewoman.

The traffic on the motorway was starting to build up by the time they reached it. Robin was aware of Ellie's arms around her waist and the heat building up between her legs. When they reached the outskirts of Bury she pulled over in a lay-by. "I'll need to phone Aid to get directions." Ellie hopped off the bike and crouched down beside it to pee. Robin moved away to speak to Aiden and give her some privacy. By the time she finished Ellie was back on the bike.

"Okay. Sounds easy enough. It's signposted once we're in the town centre. Still no news on her condition, though."

They found Aiden seated outside the maternity ward looking extremely uncomfortable on the small plastic chair. He stood up to greet them, relief evident on his face. Ellie gave him a hug and sat down with him. "Any news, hon?"

"They've given her some blood tests. But now they want to do an ultrasound scan." Aiden looked close to tears. "Is she going to lose it, Mum?"

Ellie rubbed his hands. "I don't know, sweetheart. But sometimes bleeding happens and they don't know why. She's a healthy lass. The scan will just be a precaution to see if everything's okay. Has she had any problems before this?"

"No. She's not said. A bit of cramp, sometimes, at night."

"Yes, well that's common enough."

Robin stood apart from mother and son. "I'll get us some coffees. Where's the canteen, Aid?"

"Go down there, turn left and then it's signposted."

She bought coffee and sandwiches for three and found her way back to Maternity after a few wrong turns and asking a cleaner. Aiden had his arm around his mother and she was holding onto his knee. They looked sweet together. She had always known there would come a time when Aiden realised his mother was there for him, no matter what. Ellie hadn't been convinced. She was sure the trauma of her leaving during his formative years would leave permanent scars. Seeing them now you wouldn't have known there had ever been a separation.

Her phone rang. It was her brother. Taking the phone outside, she answered it. "Hey, sis. What's going on at your place?"

"I thought you weren't speaking to me. After what's-her-name..."

"Oh shit. She left me anyway a few weeks later. Still, that's her loss."

"You're sounding more full of yourself than usual."

"Yeah, well, I've got some studio work doing backing tracks. It's good."

"Great."

"So, what's this I've seen on the news? Starling Hill under siege."

"It's a bit mad, yeah." Robin had scanned the article in the Sunday paper she'd seen on the kitchen table while she was putting out the cat food.

"How's Ellie doing?" Rick had always had a soft spot for Ellie.

"Okay, I guess."

"So, you doing Leeds this year?"

"Haven't really thought about it." The Leeds Festival had been a fixture on her calendar since her early teens.

"Come on! Eminem's headlining."

"Yeah, well. Things going on at the farm. I'll let you know."

"Okay. Look, I'll pop over one evening. We can catch up."

"Yeah, good."

"I've missed you, Rob. You might be a pain in the butt sometimes, but I still love you."

"Thanks, Rick. And I'm sorry about, you know…"

"Forget it. I've moved on. Catch you soon, kid."

She stared at the phone before putting it back in her pocket. Where had that come from? Still, it was good to know someone in her life didn't think she was a waste of space.

†

Jo arrived in the kitchen to find Tina already munching on toast.

"There's a note here. From Robin. Says she's had to go to Bury and will call you later."

"Bury? That's odd. She's never mentioned Bury although I think her brother lives in Bolton or Blackburn. One of the B towns anyway." Jo took the note and read it. "Oh well. All will be revealed, in due course no doubt. Has Harry been out yet?"

"Yeah. He's done his business. I wasn't sure what he gets for breakfast though."

"Did you have a dog at home?"

"Yeah. Brandy." Tina's eyes welled up with tears. "At least she loved me."

"Hey." Jo sat down. "I know things don't seem great now, but it will all look different in a few weeks' time. And in ten years none of this will matter."

"Ten years!"

"Well, that's what my dad told me when we moved to Germany. I was in Year 5 and had one special friend at school. I cried and cried when we had to leave. I was only ten and I couldn't even imagine being alive in ten years' time."

"Do your parents know about you?"

"No. I decided to stick to the don't ask don't tell policy. They're more concerned about my lack of career these days. Speaking of careers, I thought we could hit a few of the cafés in town today if you're still up for looking for work."

"Should I cover up my tats?"

"It's up to you. But, honestly, your tattoos won't be an issue here."

✝

Kathryn's alarm woke her from a deep sleep. She had tossed and turned most of the night and the last time she'd looked at the clock it was five thirty, and she was planning to get up at six.

The events of the day before crowded into her mind. Getting off the train at Leeds her only thought had been to retrieve her car and drive home for a soothing bath and several glasses of wine. She was aware of Den keeping pace with her along the platform but had avoided eye contact. There was a large crowd on the concourse as she cleared the ticket barrier. Cameras flashed and several voices called out, "Look this way, Professor?" and "How many skeletons are there at Starling Hill?" and the like.

Kathryn looked around for Den. "Is this your doing?"

"No. I guess word's got around, though."

"Well, I think you've done more than enough damage so you can get me out of here, now!"

Denise shrugged, and then said, "Okay. Stick close." With that she took hold of Kathryn by the elbow and started to shove her way through the throng. "No comment for now, folks. Press conference later."

They reached her car safely and Kathryn had been too shaken to object when Den climbed into the passenger seat. Once she had negotiated her way out of the city centre and reached the motorway she turned to the journalist and said, "What press conference?"

"Well, it's the best way to get your message across without being continuously shouted at."

"I didn't plan to give any messages."

"The cat's out of the fucking bag, Kathryn. You can't stuff it back in. You're going to have to talk to the press sometime."

"I talked to you, and look where it's got me."

"Look, I had no idea it would get this big. Archaeology as front-page news. A few skeletons in a field. Who knew? I was just humouring Jas."

Kathryn had maintained silence then until they reached Huddersfield. She parked in front of the train station. "This is where you get out," she said to Denise, not looking at her.

"You're kidding."

"I'm not. You can either get a train to wherever you like, or find a hotel room here. I don't care either way."

"Kathryn! I do care about you. Can't we talk about this?"

"Maybe sometime. But not right now. Just get out, please."

Den had got out then, untangling her long legs and collecting her bags. She'd slammed the door and stood watching as Kathryn pulled away. In her rearview mirror, as she waited for the lights to change, Kathryn saw her staring around with a lost look on her face. She almost turned back.

Getting home hadn't been quite the relief she'd thought she would feel. Already feeling guilty about abandoning Denise, she found a dozen messages on her answerphone. One from the dean, six from Aimee, several hang-ups, two from Ed, but then she had spoken to him on the train. He had been able to reassure her that security was in place at the farm and that he'd spoken to Ellie himself. She hadn't wanted anyone to stay with her.

Kicking off her shoes, she poured herself a generous glass of red wine and collapsed on the sofa. Pulling the phone towards her, she listened to the messages again. The dean wanted to see her at eight o'clock sharp on Monday morning. Aimee wanted to know where Tina Morris was and why she hadn't told her about the girl's predicament. And, Ed, well he'd just left short messages telling her she was an idiot, several times, only in more forceful language.

She could ignore Aimee's calls but she couldn't ignore the dean. However, there was no way she could be in her office on Monday morning. She had to meet the two archaeologists she'd drafted in to help with the dig.

Two cups of coffee and a hot shower later, Kathryn felt ready to face the day. The call to the dean the night before had been exhausting. The woman was incandescent. The university had a perfectly good public relations team. Why hadn't Kathryn gone through the proper channels? The budget had spiralled out of control. She was tempted to pull the plug on the whole project. It had taken Kathryn an hour to talk her down. She pointed out that the university was getting a lot of free publicity, the archaeology courses would be oversubscribed for the foreseeable future, and she had already secured a grant from the National Trust. English Heritage wanted in on the act as well. Paraphrasing Denise she had told her the cat was well and truly out of the bag.

The phone rang just as she was heading out the door. Hoping it wasn't the dean again, Kathryn dropped her keys on the table and picked up. It was Ed.

"Just thought you should know, there's now a police roadblock on the road leading to the farm."

"Jesus! What's happened? Is Ellie okay?"

"I should think so. There are police officers everywhere. It seems they had to respond to calls from the locals who couldn't get through with the media vans parked up. You know what that road's like. Anyway, it's just as well they turned up. Some of the twits were trying to reach the site over the fields. I don't think Eleanor's neighbours are too impressed with all this activity."

"Okay. Thanks for letting me know. And, I really am sorry, Ed. I had no idea this was going to happen. I'll be there as soon as I can. I'm picking up Phil and Ros."

"Okay. Oh, and you know Aimee's on the warpath as well?"

"Yes. I'll talk to her later."

"Good luck. You'll need it." With that, he rang off.

Kathryn grimaced at her reflection in the hall mirror. This day looked like a long one. And she still didn't know how she was going to be able to face Ellie.

†

The ride back from Bury hadn't been as hair-raising as the early morning dash. Robin had suggested stopping for lunch and Ellie was happy to agree. She couldn't face the thought of going back to the farm just yet.

They had finally been able to see Sophie midmorning. The scan had shown that everything was fine with the baby. The doctor wanted her to stay in overnight for observation. The bleeding didn't seem to indicate any serious problems, but they would know more when they had the results of all the tests. Aiden was going to stay with her as long as he could.

Robin sat opposite her at the picnic table by the canal. Ellie had the view of the waterway and the stream of walkers. They had eaten their meals in silence. "Oh my God!" Ellie clapped her hands to her head. "The cats. They'll be starving."

"I put their food out this morning, while you were getting dressed. And water."

"You did?"

Robin nodded.

"Thanks." Ellie felt tears starting. She didn't want to cry in front of Robin. "I don't think I can ever thank you enough for today."

Robin was looking down the canal path. She seemed close to tears herself when she looked back at Ellie. "Want to go for a walk?"

"Okay."

They set off along the path, not touching. After a few minutes, Robin started to talk, her voice low. "I don't blame you. I mean, I know I've hurt you. And Kathryn's a much nicer person. You're better suited, intellectually anyway. I don't know what you ever saw in a high school dropout like me anyway. I've never been good enough for you."

"Rob, don't. You've given me a lot over the years. My son, for one thing." Ellie stepped aside to let a cyclist pass. "And it's as much my fault as yours. Reaching fifty scared me. My parents both died in their early fifties. I pushed you away. You don't want to be stuck looking after an old crock, do you?"

"Ellie, you're not an old crock."

"Well, not yet, maybe. But it's all downhill from here. What is there to look forward to? Failing eyesight, loss of hearing, dementia, incontinence, arthritis."

Robin took her hand then. "Stop it. It's no good thinking that way. None of us know what's around the corner." They continued down the path, occasionally overtaken by joggers, cyclists, or other walkers. Robin let go of her hand then tentatively put an arm around her shoulders. Ellie sighed and leant into her. For the first time in weeks, she felt at peace.

"It's not what you think," she said after a while. "With Kathryn."

Robin stopped, letting go of her. "She did stay the other night, didn't she?"

"Yes. But I, well, it wasn't fair to her. I wanted it to be you."

"Do you really mean that?" Robin's eyes had welled up again. "I don't think I can bear it if you push me away again."

"I do mean it. These last few weeks have been hell. I wanted you back as soon as you'd left."

They were standing in the middle of the path, toe to toe. Robin leant down so that their foreheads were touching. She grasped both of Ellie's hands. "I know you might not believe this, but I don't want anyone else."

"I'm not going to ask you to make any promises you can't keep. I just want you with me now."

Robin pulled her closer and they kissed, gently at first, then with more urgency.

A shout of "Get a room!" from a passing cyclist brought them to their senses.

"Want to come back to my place? Jo and Tina should be out job hunting."

"Sounds good to me. Race you to the bike."

Ellie heard Robin's laughter as she took off running. She was grinning widely herself experiencing a feeling of joy she thought had been lost to her forever.

†

Kieran arrived at the roadblock. The phone call from Tommy had alerted him to the developments at the farm. He'd had to hear the news from his son living on the other side of the world. The officer was telling him they couldn't let him through, as he wasn't on their list of residents in the area. Just then another car pulled up and Kieran saw Ed get out. He called over, "It's okay. He's with the uni."

The policeman acknowledged Ed and waved both cars through. When they arrived at the farmyard, Kieran thanked the academic. "No problem. I figured Eleanor could use a friend up here today."

"When did all this kick off? And before you say it, no I don't watch television or read newspapers or surf the net."

Ed smiled. "I envy you. Well, it seems Kathryn's visit to London included giving an in-depth interview to a reporter for one of the main nationals, and also doing a television interview. That would have been fine, if the fifty people who normally watch the show on Sunday morning had just been seen it. But someone put it on YouTube, and within hours it went viral, as they say. Now this doesn't normally happen to university professors. That kind of instant fame is usually reserved for preadolescents making pop videos in their bedrooms or piano-playing cats."

Kieran laughed. "Well, I heard the news from my son in Australia. He'd seen the YouTube video. I'll go and see how Ellie's doing."

The next surprise of the day was finding out from the officer at the door that Miss Winters wasn't there. Even more disturbing was to hear that she had gone off with another person on a bike in the early hours of the morning. The officer wasn't going to let him go in the house but he convinced her he was a friend of the family and would need to see to feeding the cats.

Soames only opened one eye from his place on the kitchen window ledge. It didn't look like he was starving. Checking the bin, he saw that there was a freshly discarded tin of cat food. So, Ellie had fed them before she left. Why would she have gone off with Robin? He thought she had finished with her. It didn't make sense. Unless she had called Robin because she didn't want to be alone on the farm. But she could have called him. He was only down in the valley, less than ten minutes away.

Going into the living room he saw the phone had been left off the hook. He was about to replace it, then realised why it would be off. The media intrusion. She must have been terrified.

The next job was to look in on the hens. He collected the day's eggs and made sure they had feed as well. Then it was time to check out the studio. He had just reached the door of the old stables when the professor's car pulled up. She had two passengers, a man and a woman, both dressed for a day's digging it looked like. The man was wearing a battered sweat-stained Tilly hat. He was sure he'd seen him somewhere before. He waved, but Dr Moss didn't acknowledge his presence. She took her visitors straight over to the field where they disappeared from view behind the portable toilets.

The university coach arriving and disgorging the student workers diverted his attention then. They disappeared onto the field, chattering away in groups of twos or threes. And just behind the coach, another vehicle appeared. The young woman who got out didn't look like one of the diggers. She looked like she was dressed to go out on the town, or undressed, as Kieran always thought to himself when he saw the youngsters in the town centre on the occasional Friday nights when he ventured out to meet his mates to sink a few pints.

"Hi," she called out to him. "Have you seen Dr Moss?"

"Yes. She arrived a few minutes ago."

The woman stalked off towards the field in her fashionable—but totally unsuitable for farm wear—high-heeled sandals. Kieran shrugged and went into the pottery studio. Something else that was none of his business. Looking around at the clutter in the studio, it was clear that Ellie wasn't herself these days. It was a mess. Normally she was obsessively tidy. And then there were the cracked pots lined up next to the kiln. Another sign that she was disturbed. In all the years they had worked together, he'd never known her to misfire any of her creations. Moving the bin into the centre of the room, Kieran started to tidy up.

Having disposed of the larger items, he decided to sweep the floor as well. It was something Ellie would have done at the end of any session, but it looked like it hadn't been done for days. He was by the door when he heard a raised voice. It was the girl he had seen earlier.

"The parents are raising a stink. Their kid's gone missing and we're responsible."

"She's eighteen years old. And her story is they threw her out. It's up to her if she wants to contact them." Kieran recognised the measured tones of Professor Doctor Moss.

157

"You have no idea, do you? Just bury your head in a hole, and I'm not talking about trenches."

"Keep your voice down. And making personal comments isn't helpful."

"So, who is it you're screwing now? The delectable milkmaid or that butch-looking reporter who seemed to be gallantly protecting you from the massed media pack yesterday?"

"Aimee, I thought you came here to talk about an allegedly missing student. My private life has nothing to do with you or anyone else."

"Aha! I knew it. Fuck and tell. I wondered where all the in-depth info came from. Simon was spitting tacks when he saw it yesterday. Why did he have to read in a Sunday paper details of the dig that's on his doorstep? And an article from some city hack who wouldn't know where Huddersfield was without looking on a map."

"I've spoken to Simon. He was a bit upset, yes. But he's agreed to set up a press conference for this afternoon. So, I've made my peace with the university's public relations department and the dean. As for Tina Morris's parents, you can tell them that she is safe and well and will contact them when she feels she wants to. In the meantime they might want to think about how they can support their daughter rather than calling her a freak, among other things, and throwing her out of the house in the middle of the night. Now, I would appreciate it if you would go back to your nice little office and let me get on with my work."

Kieran decided now was the time to make his presence known. He ambled out into the yard, sweeping the debris from the studio floor in front of him. "Morning, ladies."

Two equally startled faces turned towards him. The one he now knew was called Aimee gave him a murderous glare, which he suspected had been turned on the professor

158

moments before. She then turned on her, miraculously still intact, heels and tottered off to her car.

The professor looked at him sternly from behind her glasses reminding him of a Sunday school teacher from long ago. She was wondering, no doubt, how much of the conversation he'd heard. He smiled at her. "Another nice day for it, Professor."

She nodded, and then surprised him by asking, "Is Ellie around?"

"Um, no. Seems she had an early morning appointment."

"Oh. How did she get there? Both her vehicles are here."

Kieran looked around, as if that hadn't occurred to him. The Jeep and the Corsa were parked in their usual spots. "I don't know. Maybe someone collected her."

She gave him another teacher-like stare as if she knew he knew the right answer to the question but was being deliberately obtuse. Aimee's car passed them, gaining speed as she gunned it down the track. They both stared after it. Kathryn broke the silence first.

"Okay. Well, when she comes back, could you let her know I'd like to speak with her?"

"Of course."

She went back to the field and Kieran carried on sweeping. His phone buzzed from his back pocket. Checking the number it wasn't one he knew but considering all the strange events of the day so far he answered it. And was glad he did.

"Ellie! Where the heck are you?" He listened while she told him about the early morning trip to Bury. "But it's fine? She's been properly checked out?" He knew only too well the anxieties experienced by first-time parents...and grandparents. Ellie assured him that Sophie and baby were okay. She wasn't sure about Aiden. He'd had a bad scare. She thought perhaps she hadn't been helpful telling him this was just the start. He would never stop worrying. Kieran picked up on the lift in Ellie's voice.

"Where are you now?"

She told him she was in Hebden Bridge and might be staying the night. That was where Jo lived, he recalled. But where did Robin fit in? It had to be her on the bike. He decided not to ask. It wasn't any of his business. He reassured her that everything was under control at the farm. It only occurred to him after ending the call that she had probably been using Robin's phone.

†

Robin took the phone from Ellie and placed it on the bedside table. Her other arm was still around Ellie's shoulders. She pulled her close again, delighting in the feel of Ellie's soft fair hair on her skin.

"Did he ask about me?"

"No. But I'm sure he'll figure it out. He seemed more concerned about Sophie and the baby. Anyway, I'm glad he's there."

"How did he get past the roadblock?"

"I don't know. Maybe he convinced them he was with the uni team." Ellie moved her body closer and Robin gasped as she felt the moist warmth between her lover's legs as she maneuvered them on top of her own. "Have I ever told you how much you turn me on?" she murmured seductively.

"You don't have to tell me." Robin kissed her firmly and moved her arms to grasp Ellie's buttocks. Their initial lovemaking earlier had been joyously gentle, reacquainting themselves with the tenderest parts of each other's bodies. Now, Robin sensed that Ellie wanted something more intense. And she didn't disappoint, squealing with delight as Robin spread her cheeks and slid the fingers of one hand into her wet opening from behind. Bringing Ellie to orgasm was something she knew she excelled in but the added challenge was to make her scream. The first time it had happened she had been amazed. Ellie had seemed to be so contained when they first met.

†

They had walked back to the house up the steep hill and Jo was pleased to find she was fitter than the younger woman. Tina was gasping before they reached the first level. Harry had bounded on ahead. She called him back and waited until Tina had caught her breath before continuing the rest of the climb.

"Looks like Robin's back," she said, when they reached the house. The bike was parked by the van and looked dusty, like it had been ridden hard. Jo had discovered that while most aspects of Robin's life were a disorganised mess, she looked after her bike as carefully as if it was a live being. They rounded the corner of the house to let Harry into the garden and enter through the kitchen door, and were greeted by a piercing scream followed by a loud "Oh God! Don't stop. More! There! Ahhh!"

"Sounds like Robin's pulled. Jesus! I hope the neighbours are out." Jo pushed Tina ahead of her into the house.

Tina stood gazing up at the ceiling, a look of wonder on her face.

"Well, I don't know about you, but I'd like a brew." Jo put the kettle on and got some mugs out. They'd had a tiring morning of going in and out of shops and cafés to see if there were any openings without success. Then when Jo left her at the pub to fetch Harry she returned to find her deep in conversation with Jed from the market. He seemed quite taken with the girl and had offered to let her manage his stall for the next two Thursdays while he visited his daughter in

161

Skipton. Her knowledge of music and films had won him over.

"It's not much," she'd said to Tina as they headed back to the house. "But it's a start and will get you known around town. You can help me out on Wednesday as well."

"Thanks. It'll be more fun than being stuck in a shop."

"Well, it has its moments, but it can be just as boring on slow days. Still, I know what you mean. I like being out in the fresh air and watching people."

They were on their second cup of tea and Jo was telling Tina that the placemats on the table were made from fused plastic shopping bags.

"No way! They look really cool. How do you do that?"

"I'll show you if you're really interested. It's not difficult. Getting the temperature of the iron right is important, though. Otherwise you end up with a sticky mess and a ruined iron."

Robin appeared in the doorway. "Hey, any tea going? And you better not have scoffed all the biscuits."

Jo took in the change immediately. This was a different Robin to the one she'd been sharing the house with for the last two weeks. She was glowing, radiant, and grinning from ear to ear.

"Plenty of water in the kettle. And, yes, there are some biscuits left. So, who's the lucky lady, then?"

"What?"

"I mean, I don't have anything against love in the afternoon, but you might want to at least close the window next time you bring home a screamer."

Ellie arrived in the kitchen then with one towel wrapped around her body and another around her head. "Rob, is there a hairdryer anywhere?"

Jo opened her mouth again and shut it. She looked from Ellie to Robin. "Oh."

Robin was still grinning as she said, "Yeah. Jo's got one in her en-suite. You don't mind if Ellie uses it, do you, Jo?"

Jo gave Ellie an embarrassed smile. "Help yourself, Ellie. The bedroom's the first door on the left."

As soon as Ellie had gone back upstairs, Jo turned on Robin. "When did this happen? The note you left this morning said you were going to Bury. That's in the opposite direction to Starling Hill, as far as I know."

"It's a long story."

"Fine. I'm not going anywhere."

"Look. There's a lot of shit going down at the farm right now. Do you mind if Ellie stays here tonight?"

"No, of course not. What's happening at the farm?"

"If we'd bought a paper yesterday we'd know. Apparently the professor blabbed to the press and the whole place is swarming with journos. Well, it was. The university thought they could cover it with a few of their security guys, but the police had to be called in to clear the road. Complaints from the locals."

Robin made two cups of tea and sitting down at the table filled them in on events, starting with the panicked call from Aiden. Ellie came in just as she finished telling them about Sophie's condition. Wearing one of Robin's shirts that just reached past her bottom, Jo was relieved to see she was wearing knickers. That outfit, combined with the same post-coital state of euphoria on her face as her partner, made her look younger than Tina. If she could look that good when she reached fifty plus she'd be thrilled. Without the slightest trace of embarrassment, Ellie perched on Robin's knee, draping an arm around her neck. Robin supported her with one arm and kissed her lightly on the cheek.

"So, how'd the job hunting go?" asked Robin.

Tina looked startled to be addressed by this double-headed vision. Jo answered for her. "Good. Jed's given her the chance to get some experience on the market. He's going to Skipton for two weeks, so she'll be covering his stall on Thursdays. And I thought she could help me out on Wednesdays. Should give her some useful contacts."

"Am I sacked, then?"

"Yes. Well, you were hardly an asset."

"Fair enough. Good luck, Tina." She picked up a biscuit and clamped it between her teeth. Ellie latched onto the other end, oblivious to the other two at the table.

Jo stood up. "Come on, Tina. I'll show you how to make placemats. I think I'll be sick if I stay here." But she smiled when she saw the two fingers Robin raised to her behind Ellie's back.

Closing the door on the two lovers, she led Tina into the dining room, now converted to her craft workshop. Crates of various recycled materials had been brought in from the van and were lined up against one wall. She had covered the table with an old shower curtain she'd rescued from a skip.

"Are they always like that?" asked a still wide-eyed Tina.

"Robin I'd say, yes. Ellie, no. But I don't know her that well. She's always been like a teacher to me."

†

The press conference had been arranged for four o'clock and Kathryn left the site at two to give herself time to change and get back to the university to brief Simon and make sure the photos she had sent him were in the right order. She thought that calling it a press conference was a misnomer. Her plan was to provide a lecture-style presentation but Simon had warned her there might be awkward questions to fend off. She assured him she had enough experience with cocky post-graduate students to be able to cope with whatever the press pack threw at her.

With it still being the summer break they had a choice of suitable venues but decided to use the theatre in the Creative Arts Centre over the lecture hall in the Journalism and Media Building. It was the most recent addition to the campus and had all the necessary modern equipment. Satisfied that everything was set up properly, Kathryn waited in the wings while the early arrivals filtered in. Accustomed to speaking to large groups of students she wasn't nervous about speaking, but she could feel anxiety starting to build as the noise level in the auditorium grew. Taking a large sip from the bottle of water she'd brought with her, she calmed herself, breathing deeply.

At the appointed time, the lights were dimmed and Simon strode out onto the stage. Kathryn had to give him his due; he knew how to manage the audience. Using the theme music from *Doctor Who*, a series of images flashed on the full-size cinematic screen showing the start of the dig to a final montage of the most impressive finds. Leaving this on the screen, the lights came up and Simon introduced her. When she reached the lectern he said, "Dr Moss will give an update on the work achieved so far on the site and then we will take questions." He stood aside to let her take centre stage.

Using her best lecture techniques, Kathryn talked for twenty minutes on how the site had developed from the first tentative scrapings to the scale they were now just starting to comprehend. "It was a small settlement, not much bigger than the present-day farm. The evidence from the buildings found so far indicate Roman construction, but not as well built as a Roman engineer would have demanded. One of the trenches has been excavated to six feet down and we found several postholes. This would indicate earlier Iron Age habitation on the site. Starling Hill was likely on an early cross-country route not much travelled by the Roman legions but used as a handy resting place for travellers journeying between the valleys."

She finished with the statements she knew would make the headlines. "Starling Hill is without doubt the most important archaeological site found on English soil in recent times. We are uncovering a large slice of history. It has long been known that the Brigantes tribe had a base in this part of West Yorkshire. With the identification of the items of value found with the two complete skeletons buried side by side, we believe that at Starling Hill we have discovered the final resting place of Queen Cartimandua."

Simon joined her at the lectern then. "Questions, one at a time, please."

It took another forty-five minutes before they were able to wrap it up and clear the hall. Kathryn sat on the edge of the stage and finished her bottle of water. "Well, you're the professional, how do you think it went, Simon?"

"You played them like a pro, Kathryn. You've kept the Queen of the Brigantes under your hat. I wasn't expecting that and by the expressions on the faces I saw, they weren't either. You only hinted at a connection in the newspaper."

"Believe it or not, my main concern is to protect the site. It's a good thing the police are involved in security now. The place could be swarming with treasure hunters. Fortunately, I think we've uncovered most of Cazza's burial bling. The torque featured in the news article was only one of a number of grave goods buried with the remains. And they're safely in the hands of the British Museum's curators."

"Cazza?"

"That's been our code name for her. Cartimandua is a bit of a mouthful." Kathryn stood up and stretched. "Thanks for your help today, Simon. I need to get back, there's a few more hours of daylight left and our two new recruits are keen to carry on as long as they can."

They walked out of the building together into a gloriously warm summer evening. After saying their goodbyes and shaking hands, Simon set off for his office and Kathryn headed towards the car park. Her head down, thinking about the events of the day, she didn't notice the figure leaning against her car until she was a few feet away. She stopped and stared at the tall reporter slouched against the driver's door.

"Den," she said, keeping her tone as level as she could.

"Kathryn."

"What are you doing here?" She knew this was a silly question. From her vantage point on the stage she had spotted Denise as soon as she arrived in the theatre.

"I thought we could talk."

"We've done that. Now, are you going to let me get in my car or do I have to call security?"

Den gave her a winning smile. "I thought you could take me up to the site. Some photos of the royal burial ground would be great. Give me an exclusive…"

"You've had your exclusive. Move away from my car, now!"

Den stood up straight but stayed by the door. "Please, Kathryn. This would mean a lot to me."

"You're unbelievable! I thought the other night might mean something to you other than stealing information from my files. Why don't you just fuck off back to whichever slimy rock you crawled out from?"

Den had shifted far enough for Kathryn to unlock her car with her fob and open the door. She got in quickly and started the engine. The journalist was standing as still as a stone and didn't move as she drove past her.

†

Monday evening, Jasmine paced around her office. It was nine o'clock and time she was heading home. But Den had said she would call. She checked her mobile again. Nothing. No texts. No missed calls. She had cried off the after work drinks session in the pub for this.

Their last conversation had been short and to the point when Denise phoned after the press conference at the university.

"So she flipped you off, Den. What did you expect?"

"I said I was sorry. I really like her, Jas. But she won't even look at me now."

"Didn't have you down as the U-Haul type. You slept with her once and you want to move in."

"I'm not saying I want to live with her. I just would like another chance."

"You fucked her over big-time, Den. It's not going to happen."

"Right. Well, I'm heading up to the farm now. See if I can get some photos. I'd really like to talk to this Eleanor Winters as well. I'll call you later."

That had been three hours ago. Even if she'd got stuck on ring-road hell she would have reached the farm well before now. And her mobile seemed to be switched off, not even going to answer phone.

Still worried, but deciding that Den was a grown up and would call her when she could, she switched out the lights, locked the door and made her way home.

# Chapter Eight

## Retributions

It was late on Tuesday morning when they arrived back at the farm. They had travelled in convoy to make sure Jo's van would be allowed through the roadblock. Even though they were making a late start Ellie had told Jo she would carry on with the pottery lesson planned for the day. Tina had decided to come along with Jo rather than stay at the house on her own. So that meant Harry had to come too.

It was another scorcher of a day. Ellie enjoyed the slower pace of the ride around the narrow lanes and feeling Robin's heat as she worked her hands under her shirt to hold on. She wasn't sure how much time she would be able to give Jo. Robin's response to her touch was immediate and although they had spent most of the last twenty-four hours making love, she knew she wanted more. It was as if her world had shrunk to this moment in time with her lover and there was no other reason for being alive. And so very much alive!

They stopped at the roadblock and Ellie removed her helmet to speak to the police officer. She explained that the occupants of the colourfully painted van behind were her pottery students. The officer, sweltering in the heat, just nodded and waved them through.

She only had one thought in her mind when Robin stopped the bike in front of the house. "Time for a quickie while Jo sets things up in the studio?"

Robin's grin affirmed her desire. She grabbed her hand and pulled her through the front door. And stopped.

Kieran was sprawled across the sofa, bottle of beer in one hand, TV remote in the other. Soames was lying on his stomach and Fleur had draped herself across the back of the sofa near his head.

"Kieran!"

His head swivelled round and both cats looked her way as well. "Ellie. Hey, good to see you. Oh, hi, Robin." He swung his feet onto the floor and sat up. Soames meowed in protest and stalked off in disgust at being unceremoniously dumped.

"What are you doing here?"

"Well, thanks, Kieran, for cleaning up the studio, feeding the cats this morning, letting out the hens and collecting the eggs. Apologies for not hoovering the living room, but the kitchen is fairly tidy."

"Sorry. I just didn't expect to see you here. But thank you for doing all that," she said contritely, sitting down next to him.

"Is there any more beer?" asked Robin.

"Yes. The fridge is pretty well stocked."

Robin went into the kitchen and came out with four bottles. Jo and Tina had just arrived so she passed them one each, then perched on the end of the sofa next to Ellie.

"So, what's been happening here? It looks pretty busy out there," Jo said.

"You guys didn't see the news yesterday?" Kieran asked, looking at the newcomers.

"No, we were all otherwise engaged." Jo managed not to look at Ellie and Robin when she said this.

"The professor's press conference was the main event on the local news, and even made the second item on the national."

"The story's already been in the Sunday paper. What was newsworthy about it?" asked Ellie.

"Queen Cartimandua," Tina piped up.

They all looked at her.

"One of my mates texted me. Dr Moss says that the Queen of the Brigantes was buried here."

"Why is that big news?" asked Robin.

"Well, they never knew what happened to her. Once she lost power and the Romans ditched her, she just sort of faded out of view. And, anyway she was never a hero like Boudica who kicked ass. Cartimandua sucked up to the Romans and has generally been seen as a traitor by the other British tribes."

"Wow, Tina. The professor will be pleased. You must have been paying attention in class." Robin swigged some of her beer.

Ellie groaned. "I can't believe this is happening. I thought they would just find a few bits of wall, some trinkets and coins. Then cover it all up again."

Kieran cleared his throat. "Yes, well, you've also had a visit from some bloke saying he was with English Heritage. He wants to talk to you."

"Oh shit. They've called before. They want to buy the farm. I should have let NewGen cover the place in wind turbines when I had the chance." She tightened her hold on Robin's knee.

"You can't mean that, Ellie," said Kieran. "You taught Roman history. The professor said this is, and I quote, 'the most important find on English soil in recent times.' Aren't you excited, even a little bit? It's here. On your land."

"If I'd known it was going to become a major event, I would never have agreed to them digging here in the first place."

†

Kieran had taken Jo and Tina out to the studio, after taking the hint that Robin and Ellie wanted some time alone.

As soon as they had gone, Robin slid down onto the sofa and took Ellie in her arms, dismayed to find she was shaking. "It'll be okay. Everything will settle down soon." Her words and the close contact calmed her lover.

Then just when she had moved in for a kiss, her phone rang. She groped around and dug it out of her pocket. The caller was Jasmine. She declined the call. Then she noticed she had four missed calls, all in the space of half an hour. Clicking through, they were all from Jas. "Sorry, love. I better see what she wants," she murmured apologetically to Ellie.

"Hey, what's up?" she said when Jasmine answered.

"I'm worried about Denise."

"Who?"

"Denise Sullivan. She's a journalist, a friend, the one who wrote the article for the Sunday paper."

"So, why are you worried about her?"

"She's disappeared. I mean, she said she would call me yesterday. I'm not getting anything on her phone. I checked with the hotel and she didn't come back last night." Jasmine sounded panicky.

"Maybe she got lucky."

"Not likely. Anyway she said she was going up to Starling Hill. You haven't seen her, have you?"

"We just got back here ourselves, but I can check with the diggers."

"Okay. Thanks. You'll let me know, won't you?"

"Yeah, sure. I'll see what we can find out." She ended the call and turned to Ellie. "Do you know a Denise Sullivan?"

"No. Who is she?"

"A journalist friend of Jasmine's. She's worried because the last she heard from her she was coming here. And that was yesterday." Seeing the look on Ellie's face, she added, "Don't worry. I'll go and talk to the prof."

Leaving Ellie with Soames who had been waiting to pounce on her lap as soon as Robin got up, she made her way out to the field. The level of activity had certainly intensified since she'd last seen it. There were bodies everywhere. She couldn't see Kathryn but after another scan she saw Ed's tall figure by the nearest trench.

"Hey, Dr Ed!"

He turned and smiled when he saw her. "Hey, yourself. Haven't seen you around for a while."

"Yeah. Well, just needed a bit of a break. Is the boss lady here?"

Ed looked around. "Hm. Last I saw she was down there." He pointed to the far corner of the field.

"Okay. Thanks."

"Is there a problem?"

"Not sure yet. Just need to check something out with her."

Kathryn was deep in discussion with a scruffy-looking man wearing a battered old hat. Indiana Jones come to life.

"Excuse me, Professor." Robin decided it would be best to try for politeness.

Kathryn's gaze shifted to her and her stance immediately stiffened. Robin smiled but quickly realised it was wasted on the professor so she came straight to the point. "I've just had a call from Jasmine Pepper. She's concerned about a friend of hers, Denise Sullivan. Seemed to think you might know of her whereabouts." Whatever reaction Robin had expected, it wasn't the one she observed. The professor seemed to visibly pale in front of her. She took her by the arm and moved her out of earshot of the nearby workers.

"So, have you seen her?" Robin asked.

"Not since yesterday afternoon."

"Where was that?"

Kathryn licked her lips. "At the university, after the press conference."

"And did she say where she was going?"

"No. But she did want me to bring her up here."

"And you didn't?"

"No. I told her, in no uncertain terms, to stop bothering me."

"I see."

"I doubt that. With any luck she's crawled back to London."

Interested in the venom in the professor's tone, Robin persisted. "Jas can't get through on her phone. And she was expecting her to call."

"I don't see that a missing journalist is any concern of mine."

"No, of course not. You just carry on digging up the past." Robin walked off, wondering what had rattled the usually serene exterior of Professor Doctor Kathryn Moss. Back in the farmyard, she stopped by the hens' enclosure. They were pecking away with their usual intent. She called Jasmine. "No joy. What's up between your friend and the professor?"

"It's a long story."

"So, I'm not going anywhere."

"Den got a bit carried away. She just wants to make a name for herself and this is turning out to be a big story."

"And...?"

"And, well, she appropriated some files."

"Come on, Jas. This is me you're talking to."

"Okay. They met for dinner and one thing led to another..."

"Fuck! No wonder the good doctor's pissed off with her."

"I know, and Den knows she's screwed up any chance of a relationship, but right now I'm worried about whether she's alive or dead."

"Right. Did she have a car?"

"She hired one."

"What's the last thing she said to you when you spoke yesterday?"

"She said she was going up to the farm to take photos and she wanted to speak to Ellie. Get her side of the story."

"Okay. Well, I don't know that the police will be that interested, as she's an adult. But if she's wandered off over these hills she could be lost for days. I have a friend who volunteers with the local Search and Rescue team and they always have to bail out idiots who go off unprepared. Try not to worry. She can't have gone too far."

"But she might be injured and if she's been out there all night…"

"Jas! There's nothing you can do right now. Just sit tight and I'll call you as soon as we find her. Tell me what she looks like."

After getting a description from Jasmine and telling her again not to worry, Robin returned to the house deep in thought. Soames and Ellie were where she had left them. She told Ellie what she'd found out. "If she drove up here she'll have had to leave her car somewhere. I'm going down the road to have a look."

"I'll come with you." Soames gave her the look that said he wasn't impressed when she jumped up, spilling him onto the floor.

They had only travelled half a mile down the road when Ellie spotted it. The car was tucked into a space in front of a gate. A local wouldn't have parked there, knowing that the farmer would need access for a tractor to the field. And the Hertz sticker in the rear window was a giveaway that it was a rental. Robin pulled in behind the car. They stowed the helmets away and walked around the vehicle. The doors were locked.

Ellie had checked out the landscape. "Shit. This is Owen's land. He's been giving me grief about the dig ever since it started. Even his wife had a go at me in the Post Office last week."

"What's it to do with him? His nearest field's at least a mile from yours."

"Says the increased traffic on the road is frightening the sheep."

"I've always thought he was a bit touched." Robin clambered over the gate and watched as Ellie turned it into a much more graceful maneuver. She took her hand. "Come on. Let's go and find this city plonker. Hope she hasn't fallen into a bog."

"She'll be okay if she's followed the sheep trails."

In normal circumstances, Robin would have enjoyed nothing more than a lively romp through an empty field with Ellie. They had spent numerous summer evenings making love outdoors with nothing between their naked bodies but open sky—safe from inquisitive peregrines—as long as they kept moving.

They crossed the first field and the next, moving steadily upwards. Owen's sheep were grazing in the top field. Then they saw the muddy green Land Rover up ahead.

"Chow time, I guess," said Robin. They could see the sheep starting to move towards the food trough, heard the whistles from the farmer and the black and white form of the sheep dog, low to the ground, rounding up the stragglers. Into this idyllic scene came a shout, followed by a loud bang and then a high-pitched scream.

"Jesus!" Robin took off at a run with Ellie close behind.

The scene that met their eyes was hard to believe. The irate farmer stood with a handgun pointing at a person lying prone fifty yards away. The sheep didn't seem to have noticed, they just kept moving towards their feeding troughs. The dog had flattened itself on the ground and lay watching its owner.

"Owen!" It was Ellie who shouted.

He turned towards her, nostrils flaring, "Stay there, you mad bitch! I'll shoot you as well."

"It's me, Ellie. Put the gun down, Owen."

The red mist faded from his eyes as he recognised her. He lowered the gun. Robin ran towards the fallen body. Without thinking, she stripped off her T-shirt and used it to staunch the flow of blood coming from the shoulder. She didn't know much about first aid, but it looked like the woman was going into shock.

"Denise! You're going to be all right. Just lie still. Okay, Denise." She had read somewhere that you should talk to someone and keep using their name. "I'm going to phone for an ambulance. Breathe."

With her free hand, she managed to get her phone out. Dialling 999 with one hand she asked for an air ambulance. "Ellie, what's the address here?"

"High Rise farm, Owen Chappell's place."

She relayed the information to the operator and looked back at the woman lying on the ground. "All right, Denise. The ambulance will be here soon."

"Can't get...ambulance...here." Her breath was ragged.

"No. You'll be getting a ride in a chopper. Great view from up there. Stay with me, Denise. You're going to be fine. Were you out here all night?"

The woman nodded.

"You're nuts. Lucky Jasmine cared enough to find out why you weren't answering your phone."

"Lost it."

Robin kept her talking and kept pressure on her shoulder. She could feel the blood seeping through the shirt. Ellie was behind her, just keeping a reassuring hand on her back.

The air ambulance arrived in a noisy blur of movement. The medics were calm and efficient. "Good job," one of them told Robin. "Guess you don't want your shirt back." He grinned, staring at her bare chest.

"Perv!"

"Here." He threw her a high-vis vest. "Not the height of fashion, but the best we can do at short notice."

Ellie climbed into the cabin. She shouted something at the pilot, then turned to Robin and yelled "Lindley A&E! And don't forget to feed the pigs!"

As the helicopter disappeared over the hill, Robin smiled at Ellie's coded message to alert the police. Ellie was full of surprises.

Robin looked around for Owen Chappell, who she found standing statue-like by his Land Rover, gun in hand, vacant look on his face.

"So, what do you want me to tell the cops, Owen? Gun went off by accident?"

He swiveled his head towards her. "She was trespassing."

"Gee, I guess she missed seeing the Trespassers Will Be Shot sign. That will go down well in court."

"Fuck off, you pussy-licking cunt!"

"Pretty accurate description, thanks. See you around, loser."

She walked away as calmly as she could and didn't start running until there was a field and two dry stone walls between them. The policeman on guard duty on the road seemed a bit bemused at first. But he'd seen the air ambulance in the distance and finally got on his radio.

"What's going on?" Kathryn demanded, as soon as Robin arrived back in the farmyard. "Was that a news helicopter?"

"Strangely enough, it's not always about you. No, they were airlifting a shooting victim. Taking her to hospital."

"Who? What?"

"Seems a local farmer didn't take too kindly to a roving reporter using his field as a shortcut."

Kathryn gasped. "Den! What happened?"

"The crazy bastard shot her."

"Oh my God! Is she…?"

"She's lost some blood, but I think she'll be okay. Ellie's gone with her to the hospital."

"Ellie…!"

"Yeah. I guess they might want to compare notes." Robin wasn't feeling too kindly towards the professor and enjoyed twisting the knife.

†

Ellie was sitting in the A&E waiting room observing the continuous chaotic hub of activity and wishing someone would turn off the TV. Then Kathryn arrived followed by a disheveled-looking Robin, still wearing the bright yellow Yorkshire Air Ambulance high-vis vest.

"How's Den?" Kathryn asked.

"Pretty good, considering. The wound's clean and didn't hit any bone. Bullet just nicked her shoulder. She's dehydrated, though, and has mild hypothermia from being out on the moor all night. So, they'll be keeping her in tonight. She should be okay to go home tomorrow, wherever that is."

"She can stay with me."

"Good. She probably shouldn't travel far until the wound's healed a bit." She looked over at Robin. "Couldn't you have changed, sweet pea?"

Robin glanced down at her attire. "I kind of like it. Anyway we need to get back pronto. The pigs still need feeding."

Ellie smiled at her. "Take me home, then."

"Ellie, wait! We need to talk." The professor had come straight from the dig. Hands still caked in dirt were held out beseechingly towards her. Some of the patients-in-waiting had turned their attention from the TV long enough to watch their exchange of words.

"You'll need to wash your hands before they let you in to see her." Ellie walked over to Robin and took her by the arm. When she looked back, Kathryn was standing in the middle of the waiting room looking distraught.

✝

"I can't believe you just went off like that on your own." Kieran glared at Robin as he said this, then turned back to Ellie. "Facing a madman with a gun."

"I've known Owen since I was able to walk. He wouldn't have shot me."

"Christ's sake, Ellie. He'd just shot an unarmed woman for no apparent good reason."

"What were we supposed to do, Kieran? Leave her to bleed to death while we went for help? That wasn't an option. And the real hero was Robin. She stopped the bleeding and kept her talking until the ambulance arrived."

Kieran noted the defiance in Ellie's tone. She was defending her lover. And there was no doubt that she and Robin had well and truly kissed and made up. It didn't make sense to him. He'd lost count of the times he'd comforted Ellie over her partner's indiscretions. That one wouldn't have got even a second chance with him.

They were all sitting around the kitchen table, the remains of an Indian takeaway surrounding them. Harry was sitting patiently by Tina's chair waiting in hope for another piece of chicken Korma. Two detectives had interviewed Robin and Ellie earlier. The participants of the dig had been spoken to and sent home for the day. Kieran, Jo, and Tina had been questioned as well, but as they had been in the studio taking turns at the pottery wheel, they hadn't seen or heard anything. They didn't even know that Robin and Ellie had gone looking for the missing journalist.

"I just reacted," said Robin. "Anyway, Ellie was braver. I wouldn't have gotten in that helicopter for anything."

"I wish I'd been there," said Tina. "We missed everything."

"Oh, Tina." Kieran looked at the teenager. "Sorry, I completely forgot about this. Your parents have reported you missing."

"What?"

"Yeah. I overheard a conversation yesterday. Someone from the university named Aimee came here to tell Dr Moss. But she told this Aimee person that as you're eighteen it's up to you if you want to contact your parents or not."

"Why would they say I was missing? My father told me I was 'no daughter of his' just before he slammed the front door in my face." Tina looked on the verge of tears. Ellie, who was sitting next to her, put a comforting arm around her shoulders.

"Maybe they've had time to think about it." Kieran patted her hand. "Parents don't always react well. Have they tried to contact you in the last few days? Called your mobile?"

"They don't know the number." She shrugged. "I got fed up with them checking on me all the time, like I'm six years old, so I changed the SIM a few months ago."

"Well, it is your call, then. If you want to speak to them."

"You could use the landline here. Block the number if you don't want them to know where you are," suggested Robin.

Kieran saw evidence of the internal struggle on the girl's face. He hadn't had any major disagreements with his son, but he had found it hard to cope with Tommy's decision to move to Australia. On the one hand he understood the boy's need to make a good life for himself, but he had been torn. Now, though, they Skyped every week and since his recent visit, he felt better about it all. He didn't feel he had been rejected. He could still play an active role in their lives.

Looking at the women around the table he knew they had all faced estrangement of some kind. Ellie had missed out on large chunks of Aiden's growing up years. Robin had left home as a teenager, so it was out of choice, although she seemed to have some sort of on/off relationship with her brother. And Jo, too, had abandoned her family in favour of a traveller's lifestyle. Maybe they weren't the best role models for this youngster, but who was he to judge?

Ellie whispered something to Tina that made her smile. On the other hand, thought Kieran, they all seemed well-adjusted adults, even Robin...well sometimes. Maybe she needed Ellie to keep her grounded.

"Anyone want coffee?" asked Jo.

"Thanks, but I think I'll be off now. See you in the morning." Kieran made his exit, thinking it would be a relief when things got back to normal on the farm.

†

Kathryn approached the bed cautiously. She hadn't been sure what to bring. Grapes were too much of a cliché and she suspected what Den would really like was a drink. She'd decided in the end the best thing she could give her was an apology.

Denise looked pale, eyes closed, lying back in the narrow hospital bed, the heavily bandaged shoulder exposed. There was a drip attached to her arm. Dehydration and hypothermia Ellie had mentioned. She sat down in the visitor's chair. Den's eyelids fluttered open.

"Kathryn." The word came out in a croak.

"Hi."

"What are you doing here?"

"I wanted to see you."

"Yeah, well, I'm not looking my best."

"Den, I'm so sorry."

"For what? You didn't know some mad fucker would take a potshot at me. And before you say anything else, I know it was stupid to try to make it to the farm on foot. The doc has already told me."

"You could have disappeared down a hole in the peat. Your body found a thousand years from now perfectly preserved."

"You'd have liked that. Something else to add to your portfolio."

Kathryn stared at her.

"Yeah, I saw your application to Cambridge. And no, I didn't copy it."

"Look, Den. I'm trying to make peace here. They're letting you out tomorrow. You can stay at my house while you recuperate. It's not far from here."

Den grimaced. "Could you pass me the water?"

Kathryn looked around and saw the water glass on the cabinet. She handed it to Den and watched her take a few sips.

"It's not such a bad idea, is it? I have two bedrooms. You'll have your own space."

"I've got a better idea. And I'd say you owe me."

Kathryn listened as Den told her what she wanted. She shook her head. Just when she thought this day couldn't get any worse.

## Chapter Nine

### Reconciliations

Ellie awoke to the sound of rain hitting the windows. An unfamiliar sound after the long dry spell. She reached across and found the space next to her empty. Opening her eyes, she saw a faint outline leaning against the window frame.

"Rob!"

"It's beautiful out there. Come and look." Ellie pulled on a T-shirt before joining her lover. Robin put an arm around her and kissed the top of her head. "Look at the way the mist is curling around the buildings."

It was an eerie scene. She shivered and pulled Robin's body close to hers. "The window needs cleaning."

"Is that why you want me back?"

"Of course. And after the windows, there's the henhouse to scrub down..." Laughing, she ducked under Robin's arm and ran back to the bed.

Taking one last look out the window, Robin joined her, snuggling under the duvet. "Ellie?" Feeling safe in Robin's arms again, Ellie noted the change of tone.

"Mm."

"Do you want to stay here?"

"In bed? Definitely. Indefinitely."

"No, I mean here, at the farm. Would you seriously consider selling up?"

"I don't know. Generations of my family have lived here. But I'm the last. Aiden's not interested. And now, well, it will never be the same. With all the attention this site will get from now on, it will be like being an animal in a zoo. People coming to gawk. Just think, all those years we've been walking over the graves of long dead Britons, Roman soldiers, and possibly the bones of Queen Cartimandua herself."

They lay together, silently. Ellie enjoyed the warmth emanating from Robin's body, their legs entwined. She was drifting off to sleep again, when Robin spoke again.

"What would you like to do if money was no object?"

She didn't have to think long about the answer. She had done a lot of thinking recently. "Travel. Do you know I've never been to Rome? I taught Roman history for ten years. And there are lots of other places I would like to see. I'd like to take the trans-Siberian Express from Moscow to Beijing. Travel in style on the Golden Eagle."

Robin hugged her. "You never cease to amaze me."

"But I don't want to do any of these things unless you're with me."

"Count me in. But what about the cats?"

"Yes, well, there's the rub. And how could I leave Juno, Ceres, Aurora, Venus, Flora, Fortuna, Diana, Bellona, Minerva, Luna, Apollo, and Jupiter." Ellie laughed at Robin's expression as she quickly rattled off the names of all the hens and the roosters.

"How do you do that? I can never name more than three at a time. I bet you can even tell them apart."

"Of course. They all have personalities." She rolled herself around to face her lover. "Now are you going to let me have a little snooze or were you planning to ravish me…again."

The tip of Robin's tongue finding her earlobe was all the answer required.

✝

The drive up to the farm had never seemed so long. Kathryn tried to formulate the words she would say to Ellie, concentrate on the driving, and ignore her passenger. She was only succeeding on one level, driving carefully to minimise any sudden turns or bumps in the road. The early rain had cleared off but it was still misty on the tops.

Den had stretched herself out as far as the seat would allow. It might have been the effect of the painkillers, but she hadn't said a word since leaving the hospital. The day before, Kathryn had collected her belongings from the hotel, so she had been able to bring the patient a change of clothes and her laptop.

The last person she wanted to see was naturally the first. Robin was emerging from the henhouse with a basket of fresh eggs when Kathryn brought the car to a steady stop outside the farmhouse. She walked around the car to open the door for Denise. With her left arm in a sling, she was having difficulty doing it herself.

Den looked at Robin as she approached, and recognising her, she smiled and held out her right hand. "Hey, I think I owe you a T-shirt. And thanks for saving my life, by the way."

"No problem. Just don't make a habit of wandering off over t'moors." Robin shifted the basket to her other arm to shake Denise's hand. "I don't believe we've been formally introduced. Denise Sullivan, I presume."

"Correct."

"Robin Fanshawe."

"Is Ellie in?" Kathryn asked, perhaps a little too abruptly, forgetting in that instant the reconciliation she had been working up to for the last few days. Robin gave her a piercing look that didn't bode well for a peaceful discussion, but her voice was calm when she spoke.

"Yes. Of course. We were just going to have breakfast. Walk this way."

Kathryn and Denise followed her into the house. The smell of freshly brewed coffee wafted out of the kitchen. Robin set the egg basket down on the counter and moved up behind Ellie, who hadn't turned from the chopping board when they came in. Kathryn experienced a jolt of desire as she watched Robin wrap an arm around Ellie's waist and whisper some words into her ear. She could feel the softness of her hair against her lips and breathe in the scent of her skin, a heady mixture of soap and earthiness.

Ellie turned around, with Robin still managing to encircle the smaller woman with her arms. Kathryn had to admit that they looked good together, like they belonged to each other. And the look on Ellie's face was one she hadn't seen before. Contentment wasn't quite the right word; there was a radiance about her, an aliveness.

"Sorry to barge in unannounced," she said, trying to keep her voice steady. "I wanted to get here before anyone else arrived today. I, well we, want to apologise for all the upset we've brought you."

Of all the things that had gone through her mind, Ellie's reaction to this statement wasn't one she had envisaged.

"Okay," she said. "Have you eaten? We're having scrambled eggs with parsley and chives. You're welcome to join us. Rob, why don't you pour the coffee?" Her lover gave her a kiss on the side of the head, eliciting a smile of pure joy, before letting go of her to comply with her request.

Kathryn took a deep breath and looked at Denise, who she was dismayed to see was entranced by the sight of the two lovers.

"Have a seat, Prof. Denise, why don't you sit here?" Robin pulled a chair out for the bemused journalist. She poured coffee and set milk and sugar on the table. Ellie started to expertly crack eggs with both hands, and Robin continued to set the table with knives and forks and napkins. She cut more bread and started toasting it when Ellie put the eggs on. The two women produced the meal with an effortless ease, evidence of the years they had spent together.

Nothing more was said while they were eating. Den sat back when she'd finished, saying, "Well that beats hospital food any day. Thank you."

"You look less peaky than you did when you arrived," said Ellie.

"You came to the hospital with me, didn't you?" asked Den. "I was a bit out of it, I'm afraid, so thank you. I really can't thank both of you enough. If you hadn't come to look for me…"

"Thank Jasmine, then. She was the one who was concerned about you." Robin looked over at Kathryn when she said this.

Kathryn looked away. This wasn't going to plan. She had wanted to speak to Ellie on her own, not with her attendant Rottweiler. So she was surprised when Den spoke up for her.

"Look, you can't lay the blame for all this on Kathryn. She wasn't going to give out any information about the value of the finds or supply photographs. All I had last week was a bare-bones article cobbled together from bits and pieces of speculation and the aerial photos Jas pinched from you, Eleanor. When we initially met up at Jas's flat last Thursday, my intention was simply to obtain some useful quotes to authenticate the article, which then would probably have been buried on a page in the paper that nobody reaches." Denise paused and looked around the table. Kathryn thought she was going to stop there, but again the journalist surprised her when she continued. "I took advantage of a situation, and I don't think Kathryn will ever forgive me, so I don't expect you will either. I stole the information from her files, copying everything on my phone, and I even accessed her emails."

Den took a gulp of coffee, aware of the stunned silence around the table. "I've had a lot of time to think about this while I was in hospital. What I did was horribly wrong. I have no defence. All I can say is, I'm sorry."

Kathryn looked down at the table. She was close to tears. She hadn't expected Denise to come clean.

Robin pushed her chair back from the table. "Anyone want more coffee?" No one answered. "Okay. Denise, I'm sure you would like to see the pottery studio. How about you and I wander over there?"

Kathryn looked up at her, then. Another unexpected action from an unexpected quarter. Robin just gave her the flicker of a smile before walking out of the kitchen, followed more slowly by Den.

†

Robin waited until they were in the studio with the door closed before saying anything. She turned to the journalist then. "If you didn't look like you've already taken a beating, I'd punch your lights out."

"Yeah. Okay. I wouldn't blame you. I feel like shit and that's not just the pain talking."

Robin paced around. She felt her initial anger dissipate. "Jas told me you wanted to make a name for yourself. That this is a big story for you. I mean, how old are you? Why haven't you succeeded already?"

"I'm just a run-of-the-mill hack, really. You're right. At my age I should be getting bylines on the front page regularly. Just never seem to be in the right place at the right time."

"So, you screwed Kathryn and then stole her files. Wow! I thought I had the monopoly on being a shithead around here."

"How do you know…? Oh, I guess Jas told you that as well."

They looked at each other, and then Robin burst out laughing. When she stopped, she looked at Denise and said, "So, do you still fancy your chances with her?"

"I'd like to have a chance to find out if there's more to it. The sex was good and I enjoyed talking to her. You might not think so, but she's got a pretty wicked sense of humour."

"Yeah, well. You know she and Ellie had something going for a while."

"I sort of guessed. She was very protective of her. Certainly doesn't want me talking to her."

"Ellie can hold her own. She may not look like it, but she's very strong-minded. She'll talk to you if she wants to."

"Okay. Well, thanks for not beating me up. What kind of T-shirt would you like?"

"Oh, I think we can forget that. You can buy me a few beers sometime."

The studio door opened then and they both turned around to find Kieran staring at them. Robin greeted him brightly, "Hi, Kieran. This is Denise Sullivan, the journalist who…"

"I know who she is. You've got a nerve, young lady," he said sharply. "All the trouble you've caused…"

"Okay, Kieran. Calm down. We've been through all that already this morning. The professor's here grovelling to Ellie at this very moment. And Denise has made her apologies." She turned to Denise. "Kieran's a potter as well. He lives down in the village."

They heard the university's coach pull up outside. The students piled out in their normal fashion, some talking, and some glumly gulping coffee from cardboard containers.

"The workers have arrived. Would you like to have a look at the site, Denise?"

"Yes, that would be good, thanks."

Robin took her by the elbow, and led her out of the studio, leaving Kieran gawping after them.

✝

Ellie looked down at her hands. In her head she knew she needed to let Kathryn have her say, but in her heart she just wanted the conflicting feelings to go away. While Robin was there she had been in control of her emotions. But again, in her mind, she knew why Robin had left them on their own.

Kathryn cleared her throat and her voice sounded shaky when she spoke. "Ellie, I was upset when I left here last week. And although what Den did was wrong, I have to take the blame for letting it happen. I did want to hit back at you. But, I didn't want you to be hurt. I love you."

"No. You don't love me, Kathryn. You love the idea of being in love with me. You're more in love with the objects you find in the ground."

"Ellie, that's not true. How can you even think that? And how can you think you'll have a stable relationship with that...with Robin?"

Ellie looked up at her then. "You don't know anything about my relationship with Robin. She's my life."

"You can't rely on her? How many times has she let you down?"

"I've lost count. But none of that matters right now. I love her, I always will."

"She'll let you down again. People don't change."

Ellie stood up. She poured herself another coffee. Without looking round, she said, "Is this your idea of an apology, Kathryn?"

"No, of course not. I had a nice speech prepared. But seeing you all lovey-dovey with her has knocked me off balance. I just don't think she's right for you."

"And you think you are? What about your little fling with the reporter?" Ellie turned around then and seeing the look on Kathryn's face, she knew she'd hit a nerve. "I'm not stupid, Kathryn. You didn't need to spell it out. How else would she have gotten uninhibited access to your files? She couldn't have done all that if you just met for coffee and you went to the bathroom. So, don't go thinking you're any better than Robin. The last six months have been hell for me. I know Robin has her faults, but she has a lot of good qualities as well and over the last few weeks I've realised just why I fell in love with her in the first place. No, she hasn't changed, and probably never will, but I love her with all my heart and that's something I can't change."

Kathryn let out a long sigh and stood up. "Well, I am sorry, about all of it. The students have arrived. I'd best go out and get on with the day."

Ellie watched her go and felt suddenly drained. Something soft and furry wrapped itself around her legs. Looking down she saw Fleur looking up at her and remembered she hadn't fed the cats. She filled their bowls and, moving slowly, tidied up the breakfast dishes. She was just putting them away when Robin came in. Enveloped in her lover's arms, she felt her spirit return. "Are you okay?" Robin whispered in her ear, stroking her hair.

"Mm. I am now."

"Did she have much to say for herself?"

"Not really. She mainly thinks I should dump you."

"And will you?"

"Not on your life. You're stuck with me." She moved her head so their lips could meet. The memory of their early morning lovemaking returned and she found herself kissing her lover passionately and wanting more.

†

That went well, Kathryn thought, berating herself for her inability to think straight where Ellie was concerned. She left the house hoping to immerse herself in the mechanics of the dig, making sure the students knew what they were doing for the day. The early morning rain would have destroyed some of yesterday's work. However, as she crossed the yard, another car arrived and the sight of its occupants caused her to stop midstride. Simon and the dean, for fuck's sake!

Putting on a smile, she approached the car as they got out. Simon spoke up, "Hi, Kathryn. The dean wanted to come and see what all the fuss is about."

"Great. Good idea. You might need wellies, though. The ground will be a bit soggy today." Her smile widened at the thought of the dean's cream trousers getting splattered with mud.

"Yes, of course. That's what I thought." Simon opened the boot of his car and produced the required footwear.

Kathryn watched glumly as they changed their shoes for regulation green wellingtons. So much for that little bit of fun to lighten her mood.

Robin appeared then, with Den in tow. She glared at both of them, willing them to walk past so she would be spared having to introduce them.

"Hey, Kat, is your car open? Den wants her camera," Robin called out.

That was all she needed. These two bonding. She dug her keys out and threw them over. Robin caught them deftly and passed them to Den, who just grinned at her. The grin that had got her into so much trouble in the first place. She turned her attention to the two newcomers.

"This way, please." She ushered the dean and the PR man towards the field before they could think about introductions. She spent the next half hour escorting them around the site, answering questions and instructing students on her way. During their visit she was acutely aware of Den's movements, taking photos, talking to the excavators.

At the hospital, the day before, Den had said she thought it was the least she could do to bring her to the farm, give her the chance to take pictures, and to talk to Ellie. Kathryn had said she couldn't promise that Ellie would talk to her—she was a very private person. Den had even gone so far as to suggest she stay at the farm for a few days, at least until her shoulder was better. It wouldn't do for it to be bumped about too much going to and fro from the town.

Kathryn had thought there wasn't much danger of Ellie allowing her to stay so she had agreed that she could ask. Now, she wasn't sure it wouldn't happen. If Den and Robin had buddied up then she couldn't be sure Ellie would say no to Den staying.

She had just seen Simon and the dean off the premises when Ed arrived. She knew he'd been waiting for some lab results on the second skeleton they had found with Cazza. He checked to make sure there was no one else within earshot as he approached. "It's as we thought," he said quietly.

"You haven't told anyone?"

"No, of course not. And the lab doesn't know which grave the bones were from."

Kathryn looked towards the house. "We have to keep this to ourselves. For her sake."

"Yes. I understand that."

"Thanks, Ed. I know I can count on you."

✝

Thursday morning Robin was heading back to Hebden. She knew she could have asked Jo to bring the rest of her things from the house. There wasn't much to collect. But she had a mission, one she didn't want Ellie to know about. Jo had arrived with Harry just as they were finishing breakfast.

Before she left, Jo asked her to check on Tina, see how she was doing on Jed's stall, and Ellie asked her to pick up some veg while she was at the market.

Riding into the valley she thought she would miss the place of her exile. In spite of the despondency of her mood most of the time she'd been living there, the community atmosphere had filtered through her fog and lifted her spirits at times. But, then, it wasn't like she was leaving it behind forever. She was planning to come over for the boxing sessions as often as she could. And if Ellie did decide to sell the farm, she was sure she wouldn't take much persuading to buy a property on a bit of farmland on one of the hillsides surrounding the town. She might even want to leave the farm life behind altogether and live in a penthouse flat.

Having completed the first, and most important of her errands, and collected her belongings from the house, the final stop was the market. She saw Tina and waited while she dealt with a customer. Jo had been enthusiastic about her new assistant when she arrived at the farm earlier, telling them that Tina had a naturally easy way with customers. She didn't pressure them, but answered questions when asked, and even managed to sound knowledgeable about the various craft items on display. The stall takings had doubled in that one day.

Robin approached the music stall after the customer moved away. "Hey, kiddo. How's it going?"

Tina looked up from her money pouch. "Fantastic. I've sold seven CDs and five films so far."

"Well, I can't promise to sell anything, but I can watch the stall if you'd like a break."

"Okay, thanks. I wouldn't mind."

Robin handed her a tenner. "Could you bring me back a cappuccino? And get yourself a sandwich if you want."

Tina unbuckled the bum bag and handed it to Robin. "Just in case you do sell anything."

Robin waved her away and flipped through the CD display while she waited; nothing there she would have paid money for and the films weren't much better. She sat back on the stool and watched people walk through the stalls. Some were just browsing, the unemployed and the retired, she guessed. And then there were those who knew exactly what they wanted and just made a beeline for it. Quick in and out. Probably hadn't paid for a parking ticket and were chancing missing the traffic warden's round.

"Another job?" Michelle was grinning at her from the other side of the stall. "You looked miles away."

"Oh, hi. No, I'm just minding the stall for a few minutes. And, guess what, I'm moving back to Starling Hill."

"Gosh. You're a fast worker. Was it my pep talk that helped?"

"Helped me get my ass in gear and get some work done. No, it was a family emergency that got us together again."

"Oh. Everything okay?"

"Yeah. Just a minor scare. Ellie's son's girlfriend is pregnant. It's their first, so they're anxious about any little thing."

"I know the feeling. It is scary. Anyway, does this mean I won't be seeing you tomorrow?"

"I want to keep it up, just not sure about tomorrow. I'll text you if I can't make it."

"Great. Well, take care. See you around." Michelle disappeared into the crowd, leaving Robin to her musing.

Tina came back all smiles and handed Robin her coffee in a brightly coloured cardboard container.

"Been at the sauce?" Robin asked. "I'm sure Jo warned you about drinking on the job. She wasn't happy with me when I came back from the pub the other day." She handed the money pouch back to the girl.

"No, it's not that. I phoned home. Spoke to Mum."

"Okay. How was she?"

"Relieved to hear from me. She says they've talked about it and Dad's calmed down. He's sorry about what he did and said, and they want me to go back home."

"But…" Robin thought there was a but coming.

"I said I'd think about it. I mean, I'm happy here. I told her I thought we all needed a bit of space. It's probably time I left home anyway."

"Right. Well, that's a start. At least you know you can talk to them now." Robin took a sip of her coffee and waited, sensing there was more on Tina's mind. She didn't have to wait long.

"Um, Robin. Can I ask you something?"

"Sure."

"Is Jo, I mean, does Jo have a lover?"

"Not that I know of. There was someone she was with for a while, but she left last summer."

Tina looked at her from under her fringe. "Do you think she'd be interested in me?"

"You want me to ask her?"

The girl blushed and nodded.

"Look, you're going to have to learn how to do this yourself." Seeing Tina's disappointment, Robin took pity on her. "But, I know it's not easy, especially if it's the first time. I'll sound her out for you. Then it's up to her. Okay?"

Tina's smile came back; she positively beamed. "Thank you. You're the best."

Robin smiled. Well, at least that was someone who was easily satisfied. She left Tina as another potential customer approached the stall and went in search of vegetables.

†

Jo returned from her pottery lesson to find Tina lying on the sofa in the living room, eyes closed, listening to something on her headphones. She sat up quickly when Harry bounded over and licked her face.

"How did it go?" asked Jo.

"Okay. Jed was pleased when he came over to pack up."

"Good. I thought you would be fine. I'm going to make some pasta."

They went into the kitchen. Jo started getting out the ingredients, suggesting Tina pour them each a glass of red wine. She wasn't sure how she was going to start this conversation. When Robin told her about Tina's crush on her, she'd been taken aback.

"I've not done anything to encourage her."

"You've been kind to her."

"We both know that's not a great basis for a relationship."

"Who said anything about a relationship? I think what she needs right now is a mentor. You'd be like her spirit guide or something. Wouldn't you have liked an older woman to take you in hand, so to speak, when you were a virgin?"

"But she's so young, Robin. I'm twice her age. I could be her mother for God's sake!"

"Well, like I told her, it's up to you how you handle it. She fancies you. So, you either let her down gently, or…"

Or what? Jo had almost driven off the road several times on the way back from the farm thinking about the possibilities. Robin's suggestion that she treat it like some sort of initiation had some merit, she supposed. But she had never found sex for the sake of sex a satisfactory experience. There needed to be some spark between her and the other woman. And she hadn't felt that with Tina. She cared about her, but in the same way she cared for any wounded creature. The same way she cared for Harry. Well, maybe not quite the same way.

She still didn't know how she was going to talk to the girl as she stirred the pasta sauce. To her relief, Tina started to talk to her. She told her about phoning her mother and how she felt it was easier to talk to her because she wasn't living there. Jo could empathise with that. She explained how her relationship with her parents had eased over the years. She remembered to send them birthday and Christmas cards, and sometimes even remembered the Hallmark sponsored occasions of Mothers and Fathers days, and visited once or twice a year. But Aldershot was a long way south and she wasn't inclined to make the drive just for the sake of it.

By the time she'd finished the meal and the second glass of wine she was feeling more relaxed. She decided to ask Tina about the large tat on her left bicep. "What's with the Mallory Knox tattoo?"

"They're a band I like. Alternative rock music."

"Oh, right. Robin thought it was odd that you had the name of a serial killer on your arm. I mean, even if it was a fictional one from that movie, *Natural Born Killers*, which came out before you were born."

"Well, I haven't seen the film. But I know that's where they got the name. Anyway, I like the name, Mallory. If I had a kid, that's what I would call it. Could be a boy or girl's name, couldn't it?"

"Would you like to have kids?"

"Sure. Sometime before I'm thirty anyway."

Jo couldn't resist saying, "Anyone over thirty must seem pretty old to you."

Tina didn't even blink when she said, "It depends on the person."

Jo sighed. "Look, I don't know if this is a good idea. You're a bit young for me, Tina. Are you really interested in me? Or is it just because I'm available and you've had to see and hear Robin and Ellie making out like a pair of rabbits?"

"I really like you, Jo. And maybe it is because of Rob and Ellie. But I want to know what that feels like. To be that close with someone. I've never even kissed a woman, but I want to kiss you."

"Okay. Well, we could start with a kiss." Jo opened her arms and Tina moved in for a hug. They kissed, lightly at first, and then Jo felt her hormones take over. Maybe Robin was right. She didn't have to fall in love with the girl, just give her a memorable first experience of loving.

†

"I'll clear up. You go and chill out."

After doing the dishes, Robin made coffee. Decaf for Ellie, she only drank caffeinated in the mornings. Carrying the mugs into the living room, she found Ellie sitting in her chair listening to country music, eyes closed, foot tapping. Robin smiled. It was the Mary Gauthier album she had bought her some years ago.

"I love this," she said, taking the mug from Robin. "I'd forgotten how much. Even the songs with sad lyrics make me feel happy."

"Yeah, I know what you mean."

The last song came on and Ellie jumped up. "Dance with me."

It wasn't a slow song, but it demanded movement. They did their own version of a line dance, singing along with the chorus. When the song ended they both collapsed, laughing, onto the sofa. The cats, unimpressed with the noise and the hilarity, had left the room, tails held high.

"We should go line dancing again. I used to enjoy that," Ellie said, when she'd caught her breath.

It had been a regular Saturday night outing for several years, Robin recalled. And somewhere in the house they probably still had the outfits—cowboy boots, hats, and snap-button checked shirts.

"Why did we stop?"

"They changed the venue to somewhere on the other side of town. I don't know. We just stopped going." Robin looked at her lover, flushed from the dancing and wondered again at her own stupidity. How could she have jeopardised her life with Ellie for a night or two of fairly mindless sex with other women? Even the times with Jas had been mainly lust-filled encounters that faded with each mile she travelled north from London.

Robin stood up. If she were going to do it she would have to do it now.

"Where are you going, hon?"

"I've got a present for you. Stay right there."

"It's not my birthday."

Rummaging about in her rucksack, Robin found the folder and tucked the other item in her pocket. She sat down next to Ellie again. "Well, this is an early birthday present." She handed Ellie the folder. "It's not the Golden Eagle, but it's a start, isn't it?"

Ellie was examining the printed pages in the folder. Her eyes filled with tears. "The Orient Express! To Rome. Oh, Robin, that's wonderful."

"And it doesn't end in Rome. Instead of flying back to London from there, I thought we could hire a bike, or a car if you prefer, and go on to Florence and Venice. And then follow the coast round to Split and Dubrovnik."

"Rob, this is wonderful. But you can't afford this, can you?"

"I got paid for two jobs I finished recently. And I've got another one to do before we go." She didn't tell Ellie she was planning to sell her bike as well. That was a discussion for another day.

Ellie hugged her. "Thank you so much. I've always dreamed of doing a trip like this." She looked into Robin's eyes. "But what about…?"

"The cats, Minerva, Venus et al? Well, I thought of that. We could ask Kieran to move in for a few weeks."

"You've thought of everything. I love you." She nuzzled her neck and Robin held her close. The small round shape dug into her hip. She would ask her, but not tonight. One thing at a time. It was enough for this evening to bask in the glow of having given Ellie at least one thing she wanted. There was no rush. The Marriage Equality bill had only just been passed and the law wouldn't come into effect until the next year anyway. Plenty of time to get down on one knee and ask Ellie to marry her. In fact, she would, she decided then, do it in Rome.

"Robin?"

"Mm."

"It's only eight o'clock, but do you think we could go to bed now?"

"I should think so. Soames and Fleur have already deserted us."

# Epilogue

The archaeological dig at Starling Hill farm continued well into the start of the academic year in 2013. The finds from the grave, which were confirmed overwhelmingly by other experts as being that of Queen Cartimandua of the Brigantes, weren't as numerous as the Sutton Hoo hoard but they excited a lot of interest amongst historians. Kathryn wrote a paper that was published widely and the following year she hosted a three-part television special detailing the importance of the Starling Hill site in expanding the body of knowledge about the relationship between the British tribes and the Romans at that time. She was invited to speak at both Cambridge and Oxford and the job offers flowed in. The deciding factor on which one to accept depended on the distance she wanted to keep between her and Denise Sullivan.

Her relationship with the journalist, after the rocky start, had deepened into a friendship that she cherished but wasn't sure she wanted to take further. Whenever they were in the same city at the same time, they met up, went out for a meal and had sex. Kathryn enjoyed their encounters but she knew that she hadn't quite got Eleanor Winters out of her system. She wasn't in love with Den.

And when the invitation arrived in the spring of 2014, she had debated long and hard about whether or not to go. In the end she had called Den and asked her to go with her. She had been giving a lecture at the Museum of London so they travelled up together on the train. As it pulled out of King's

Cross, Den nudged her knee under the table. "Last time we made this journey, you asked me to sit somewhere else."

Kathryn winced. "Yes, well, you were a major aggravation."

"Are you sure you want to do this?"

"Not really." Kathryn sighed and looked out the window. "But I think it might help to see her do it with my own eyes."

The train started to pick up speed and Kathryn was aware of Den's penetrating gaze. Finally the reporter spoke, "What is it you held back, Kathryn?"

"What do you mean?"

"I've read all your stuff on the dig. Hell, I've even written a lot about it myself. But I get the feeling there's something you're not saying."

Kathryn shifted in her seat, unable to meet Den's eyes. "Ellie wanted her land back. She doesn't need more media attention. And, like so much of Cartimandua's life, it is only speculation."

"Your speculations are generally pretty accurate, I'd say."

"All right. I'll tell you a story. But, remember, it's only a story, possibly a fantasy." Den nodded and Kathryn continued, slipping easily into lecture mode. "As you know we found two skeletons side by side. The smaller one, we believe was the queen as affirmed by the value and nature of the grave goods. The taller skeleton was assumed to be that of her lover, Vellocatus. The armour plates and remains of a sword indicated that this was her husband's former armour-bearer. The one she scandalously ran off with. She disappears from history then. Off the map, completely. What happened to her? Some say she went to Chester, some say she ended up on a farm in Italy. None of this has ever been proved. So, what was she doing at Starling Hill? Why end her days on a remote hill on the edge of Brigantes territory? You have to remember she had been in power for a long time, maybe thirty years. No one knows how old she was when she became queen. She could have been fifteen, or twenty-five. What did she look like? We know she was one of the fair-haired Celts, taller than her Welsh counterparts. Her pro-Roman alliance had made her wealthy. So, even in middle age she was possibly still a beautiful and healthy woman. The story, as much as history tells us, is that she divorced or separated from her anti-Roman husband, and went off with his young armour-bearer. The fact is, and this is between me and Ed, and now you, the other skeleton found in her grave was also a woman."

"Wow. You mean…"

"Yes. It seems likely she ended her days living peacefully as a hill farmer with her female lover. And it would be wonderful to be able to give this revised version of events to the world, but I will only do that if Ellie decides to sell up."

†

Jo surveyed the trestle tables. Everything looked to be set for the reception. And the weather, for once, was playing its part. It was a beautiful clear day, with just the occasional fluffy white cloud moving majestically across the deep blue of the sky, punctuated by the occasional jet trail. As best woman it was her job to make sure nothing had been overlooked in the preparations.

Kieran came out of the house, looking very smart in white shirt and dark trousers. The occasion wasn't meant to be too formal, so he wasn't wearing a tie. His hair had grown back to the length he preferred and was tied back in a neat ponytail.

"Is she ready?"

"Yes. She looks stunning." He sighed. "I wish I wasn't giving her away."

"You're not giving her away." Jo smiled at him. "It's not a traditional wedding."

"Well, it feels like it to me."

Jo looked towards the house. "What's Tina doing?"

"Whatever it is bridesmaids do. I've left them to it."

Jo smiled again. Tina had blossomed in the last year. She was no longer the shy, unconfident teenager, hiding behind a punk persona and a curtain of hair. She still had the punk look, and definitely more attitude, but Jo knew the softer side. The few weeks they had spent together as lovers were a sweet memory. They had gone to the Leeds Festival together and bonded over the intensity of those few days of sun, sex, and rock 'n' roll. Tina had thought it would last forever, but Jo knew that it was a short-term affair. The girl went back to university when the autumn term started. They saw each other on a few weekends after that, but Tina had found her feet. She started to make friends and, as Jo had known would happen, they drifted apart. When Wade and Ian returned from their Canadian adventures, she moved into a house with two other women and had recently started seeing someone. It had only been a few dinner dates so far, but Jo felt there was something developing. She felt more settled than she'd ever felt before and was even thinking of selling the camper van and moving into a canal boat. A compromise. The boat was permanently moored to the bank but there was the constant movement of the water against the hull, hire boats passing through the lock, on their stately way to another place.

There was a car coming up the track. It was stopped by the tall figure wearing a bright yellow high-vis jacket with Yorkshire Air Ambulance lettering on the back. He directed the driver to the designated parking area.

"Dr Ed looks like he's done this before."

"Well, he volunteered for usher duty. Mind you, he's always had a soft spot for Ellie," said Kieran.

✝

Sophie looked around at the empty field. "I told you we'd be too early."

"I know. But Mum wants to see Wren before everyone else gets here." Aiden struggled to undo the straps on the car seat. Then lifted his daughter out carefully.

"Well, she won't be too pleased if she sicks up on her outfit."

"She won't. She'll be on her best behaviour today." He patted the baby on her back and she burped obligingly.

It was only two months since the first gay marriages had taken place in England with the passing of the Marriage Equality bill into law. Sophie had taken the phone call from Rome back in October, only days before Ellie's birthday. At first she couldn't take in what Ellie was telling her, there was a lot of noise in the background. It seemed that Robin had chosen the site of the Coliseum against the backdrop of tourist groups and city centre traffic to pop the question.

The intervening six months had passed in a blur—the birth of Wren in December, four days before Christmas, and then the lead-up to this wedding. She knew that Robin had tried to persuade Aiden to make it a double, but he'd said he didn't want to spoil his mother's big day. Sophie was happy for now seeing him settle into fatherhood. They might decide to get married, but he was in no rush and she figured they would probably be celebrating Wren's sixteenth birthday before he was ready to commit himself.

✝

Robin arrived with her brother, Richard. She had stayed overnight with him in Bolton and although it had been tempting to make a night of it, she had said no to staying up all night drinking. This was a once in a lifetime event and she wanted to be able to remember it.

She was wearing a summer-weight cream suit, with an open-necked white shirt. Their invitations had specified no ties and no kilts. Rick was still unattached and wanted to know if there would be any hot babes for him to chat up. Robin had assured him there would be plenty of hot women, all lesbians, before reminding him he was attending the wedding as the representative for their family and needed to behave. Her attempt at making amends with her parents at Christmas had failed. They were still saying she was a freak of nature and no child of theirs. When Rick had tried to smooth things over with them and explain that Robin was getting married their father had gone into a long rant about marriage being a sacred union between a man and a woman.

"I'll send them a photo," he'd told her when he returned from the visit. "When they see how beautiful Ellie is, they might come round."

"I won't hold my breath. Dad will just say 'what a waste.'"

The parking area was full of vehicles when they drove up the track to the farm but Ed had saved them a space near the farmyard as promised. Robin couldn't wait to see Ellie. When they had agreed to spend the night before the wedding apart, she hadn't thought it would be so difficult. Having resisted the option of drinking herself into oblivion, she suffered a sleepless night wondering why she had thought this was a good idea. It was their first night apart since their reconciliation back in August.

The field had been returfed after the dig and apart from one feature wall left exposed in the top corner, it looked like it had before, only the ground was level now, like a playing field. No more graves. The bones of Queen Cartimandua and her consort were resting in the British Museum. Talks were ongoing in archaeological communities in York and Aldborough about where the final resting place should be. Robin spotted Den's distinctive shaggy mop of hair next to the sleek groomed head of the professor. The last time she spoke to the reporter, she hadn't been sure Kathryn would come.

The guests were seated in rows, with an astro-turfed aisle down the middle, leading to the makeshift altar. The register would be signed afterwards in the pottery studio. When they had planned the guest list, she was surprised at the large number they ended up with. Ellie even wanted to invite Owen Chappell. When Den hadn't pressed charges against him, he only got a slap on the wrist for discharging a firearm and hadn't even spent a night in the police station. And just before Christmas he had come up to the farm with his wife and apologised to both of them. She could see the back of his head now, seated with some of the other neighbours, all of whom had made their peace with Ellie one way or another, after the dig had finished.

Robin saw the Hebden Bridge contingent had turned out in full including Wade and Ian, who she'd met a few times now when they went over to the other valley to have dinner with Jo and some of the boxing crew. And then there was the university crowd, students who had taken part in the excavations, and Tina's new friends. All these people here to witness this officially sanctioned union between herself and the woman she loved. She had thought there would only be the requisite two witnesses to their wedding when she had asked Ellie to marry her.

The gentle harpsichord music floated out over the hills as Robin took her place at the back of the assembled guests.

†

Ellie felt like she was floating on air. Her hair was longer now and settled over her shoulders. The light, summery dress wafted around her thighs as she stepped out of the house. Taking a deep breath, she let Kieran take her by the elbow and lead her towards the field.

The night by herself had been strange. She had thought it would be easy, having some space away from her lover before the ceremony. Time to think. But the temptation to phone Rob and ask her to come back had plagued her all evening and through her fitful sleep.

The arrival of Aiden and Sophie with her grandchild had been a welcome diversion from the morning spent with Tina, Jo, and Kieran fussing around. Wren was a beautiful child and, holding her, she thought that being a grandmother wasn't such an ordeal after all.

And now, Robin was waiting for her. She could see her as they approached the gate, looking wonderfully handsome in the suit they had chosen together. Close up she saw the nervous grin on her lover's face, the look she'd had in Rome when she proposed to her. Followed by the delighted relief when she'd said yes.

Kieran left them together to go and take his place in the front row, next to Jo and Tina.

"Do you still want to do this?" Robin whispered.

"Only if you promise to make love to me afterwards."

"That's a promise I know I can keep."

Ellie took her hand and they walked down the aisle together.

# The Last Word...

## A Voice from the Past

She had lain a long time in the cold ground, unheralded, forgotten, surrounded by a few tokens representing her position and her wealth, ill-gotten gains some would have said, including her poor excuse of a husband. What did they know? She had kept the peace, traded with the invaders. She had taken care of her people. Her tribe lived free.

Why did that bitch, Boudica, and her rabble grab all the attention? Iceni upstarts. Bunch of foul-smelling horse breeders, rampaging about the countryside, killing, looting. No better than the Romani. Numerous books were written about the marauding queen, a statue erected in a place she'd burned to the ground, and what recognition did she, the peacemaker, achieve? The occasional one line in dry historical tomes. A footnote in the history of the greatest tribe in northern Britain.

And now, her final resting place disturbed. She had chosen to retire here. Away from the conflict raging in her formerly peaceful queendom. It had been a tranquil, healing time with her lover, away from the strife, watching the starlings swoop and play in the clear air across the moors.

Ah, Vellocatus, what a pretty boy! So, they all thought. She had fooled them all, stealing away with her husband's trusted armour-bearer to live as they pleased, away from prying eyes. Together they had lain, side by side, for twenty centuries. Now, separated, each in a glass cage, she missed the closeness of her tall lover's bones.

She could dream of a time when they would be together again. When the mages of this time were done with poking and prodding, they would lie together once more. Though not on their hilltop retreat. Sturnus Colle now belonged to another golden-haired woman and her tall lover. She, Cartimandua, the Queen of the Brigantes, wished them well.

# About the Author

## Jen Silver

Jen lives in north-west England with her long-term partner and, sadly, no pets (due to allergies!). She has always enjoyed reading an eclectic range of genres including sci-fi, fantasy, historical fiction and lesbian fiction. In summer, much of her time is taken up with golf, archery and travel. To while away the long winter evenings, she started writing stories about the various lesbian communities she has experienced in London and the provinces. Her first hand experience of an archaeological dig and interest in Roman history was the creative force behind her first published novel, "Starting Over" released by Affinity in October 2014

Contact Jen at jenjsilver@yahoo.co.uk or 'friend' her on Facebook.

## Other Books from Affinity eBook Press

**Twisted Lives**—Ali Spooner A twist of fate leaves Bet and her daughter Kylie stranded at the entrance of the home of Alex Graves, as she flees the control of an abusive husband. When custom –homebuilder Alex arrives to find steam boiling from Bet's car and a beautiful child asleep in the passenger seat, her heart goes out to them. Alex offers shelter to the pair setting off a chain of events that bring both mother and daughter close to her heart and danger to her door. A heartwarming story of true love that will keep you smiling long after you've finished the book.

**Malodorous**—Del Robertson Sequel to **My Fair Maiden** Something in Fairhaven stinks. Other than the mutton stew, that is. Gwen thought life after being a virgin sacrifice would be a bed of roses. Bodhi was just looking for a wench to bed. Neither less-than-dashing hero nor not-quite-so-pure maiden imagined they would meet again, much less be trapped together in a city the likes of the ill-named Fairhaven. There's a killer on the loose. Fairhaven's on lockdown, its citizens fearful for their lives. The local guards are corrupt. And, Bodhi's been accused of murder…

**Desert Blooms**—Dannie Marsden Luce's story continues in DESERT BLOOMS… When we last met Luce Velazquez in Desert Heat, she went through hell and back to salvage her soul and reputation. Hoping to get her life back on track with lover Beth Ryan, a woman who understands her pain and can relate on every level. Instead, Luce is in the hospital, and Beth in protective custody. Jessica Sullivan, Luce's friend and ex, has big doubts about the sincerity of Beth's love, and is in no hurry to release her from custody. Can Luce's new found happiness last, or is Jessica correct in her doubts? A heart stopping romance that will fill you with the wonder of friendship, anger of betrayal, and the everlasting vision of love.

**Finding Her Way**—Riley Jefferson Is it love or just great sex? After ending an abusive marriage, Jerrica Kerrison is finally alive and she's apologizing for nothing! She has a job with a financial firm in Boston, a townhouse in Newburyport, and a sports car she drives way too fast. Jerrica has everything except that indefinable emotion called love. Madison Jeffrey is a lost soul. A PR job in the south has always protected Madison from the pressures of her family. But one day, fate brings her back to New England, forcing Madison to face her long buried demons, and a sister who despises her. When a chance meeting brings Jerrica and Madison's separate worlds crashing together, the attraction is instantaneous. After one passionate night together, Jerrica retreats into the safety of her world, leaving Madison to figure out what happened. Will Jerrica open up her heart to the idea of love? Can Madison finally believe that she is worthy of unconditional love? Or will a devil hiding in the shadows tear them apart?

**HER**—Lisa Ron Fox has been looking for that one person who will make her feel complete-her perfect match. Together with her friends, Megan and Tree, Fox continues her quest while dodging exes and clingers, laughing a lot along the way. When she meets Madeline, she instantly knows that she finds HER. Madeline has her own problems-notably a domineering husband. Can Fox win her heart? Can they make a life together? This story will make you laugh, cry, and hold your breath as the story unfolds. With the right person love can conquer all.

**Bayou Justice**—Ali Spooner   Hell hath no fury like a woman scorned. When Kara, Sasha's, new lover is taken hostage as a diversionary tactic to allow the drug dealing Bellfontaine brothers to escape justice, Sasha springs into action. Kara is released physically unharmed, however, her emotions, and budding career in the District Attorney's office are left in shambles when she is held blame for their release, Appalled, by the failure of the criminal justice system, Sasha exacts her own brand of justice for the acts committed against her lover. From the Bayou's of Louisiana to the jungles of South America, Sasha plots her revenge.

**Out of Retirement**—Erica Lawson   Melanie Stokes was a doctor—a very good one, or so she hoped. She was calm and cool under pressure, and very little fazed her. Until…Caitlin Joseph ran a small retirement home for older women in need. The fact that everyone in the house was gay was a coincidence, although it did cut down the number of women agreeing to live there. Mel took up an offer to do some relief work for a local community center when their regular doctor was away on holidays. As soon as she arrived at the home she knew something was different about the place. Was it the little old lady chasing the paper boy down the street or the sign saying "Dykes Retirement Home"? But there was something about the place that also appealed to her. Sure, Caitlin was cute as a button, but it was more the fact that she took very good care of her charges, despite their rather bizarre behavior. The older women seized the opportunity to introduce a woman into Caitlin's lonely life, using any means possible to keep Mel coming back. Their plans were boosted by the introduction of another woman into the house, who set hearts a fluttering and blood pressure rising. Now if she was a lesbian it would have been perfect...

**Letting Go**—JM Dragon A failed relationship puts Stella Hawke's life on the brink of chaos.

When her grandmother falls gravely ill in Ashville, Stella ends her army career to take care of the woman during her last weeks. Little does she know that an old army comrade, socialite Reggie Stockton, whose family owns the local newspaper, also lives in Ashville. Will she allow herself to accept Reggie's help to turn her life around and let go of the past? This is a journey where both women re-evaluate what they want out of life. Will that path lead to happiness or to a parting of the ways?

**Through the Darkness**—Erin O'Reilly Becca Cameron is a loner—by choice. She lives in a hundred year old farmhouse built by her great grandfather. A tragic accident in her home a year earlier drove away her lover, and Becca tries to accept what she cannot change and hang on to the belief that love can conquer all. Chase Hunter, had a meteoric rise in the Eastman Corporation and was, at thirty-four, the youngest vice-president. To Chase, her work was all consuming leaving little time for friends or lovers. There was simply no place in her life for anything but her job. When Becca and Chase meet at their work place, the attraction is spontaneous. Life begins to look brighter for both women as work takes a second seat to romance. Unknown to either woman, someone is watching their every move... Will passion outweigh doubt? Can love conqueror fear?

**Galveston 1900: Swept Away**—Linda Crist On September 7-8, 1900, the island of Galveston, Texas, was destroyed by a hurricane, or 'tropical cyclone', as it was called in those days. This story is a fictional account of Mattie and Rachel, two women who lived there, and their lives during the time of the 'great storm'. Forced to flee from her family at a young age, Rachel Travis finds a home and livelihood on the island of Galveston. Independent, friendly, and yet often lonely, only one other person knows the dark secret that haunts her. Madeline "Mattie" Crockett is trapped in a loveless marriage, convinced that her fate is sealed. She never dares to dream of true happiness, until Rachel Travis comes walking into her life. As emotions come to light, the storm of Mattie's marriage converges with the very real hurricane. Can they survive, and build the life they both dream of? This second edition of one of Linda Crist's best-loved novels maintains the original story, while incorporating some reader-pleasing passages that were cut from the first edition. As an added bonus, the short story "Something to Celebrate" is included at the end of the novel, detailing further adventures of Rachel and Mattie.

**Rapture: Sins of the Sinners**—A. C. Henley & Fran Heckrotte A serial killer is targeting young lesbians throughout the state of Texas. Texas Ranger Cochetta Lovejoy is assigned to the case. Convinced she knows who is committing the murders, Ranger Lovejoy is willing to do whatever it takes to put the perpetrator behind bars--even if it means stretching the limits of the law by manipulating the judicial system. Detective Agnes Kelly-Elliott is one of Ft. Worth Police Department's finest investigators. When Ranger Lovejoy appears on the crime scene of a recent murder, Agnes fears a dark secret that, if revealed, could destroy her family ties, and end her career. This is a dark, gritty, graphic tale of desire gone awry, and flawed characters looking for redemption in all the wrong places.

**Absolution**—S. Anne Gardner Games of the rich and famous, love, lust, and forbidden passions weave this tale that play out through decades and the world. The close ties the Alcalas have to the royal house of Spain provide them with an unspoken untouchable policy. Their passions and their secrets are about to come to light with a force that cannot be stopped. In this whirlwind is Cristina Uraca Alacala who is searching for a truth that has been denied to her most of her life and she must find. She is not unlike her family; Cristina does not stop until she gets what she wants. In the fog lies the truth that she must travel through to find. In this tale wealthy socialite Annais Francesca D'Autremond is a pivotal person of interest in Cristina's search for the truth. When these two women meet they find themselves drawn together by something greater than themselves. As the truth of a hidden past becomes clearer their passions grow beyond the realm of the no return instead of a status quo. Both tied together by destiny; will both survive the onslaught of past and present passions?

**Denial**—Jackie Kennedy Time spent in Somalia has Doctor Celeste Cameron accustomed to living and working in a war zone. Coming back home to America, Celeste is glad to see the end of the peril she has been in—or so she thinks. Danger seems to follow Celeste and she finds it in the shape of Amy. What Celeste feels for Amy scares her more than anything she has faced in war zones. Amy has the same feelings, but is in denial and vows to marry Josh, Celeste's twin brother, no matter what. When fate brings them together again, will they give in to their mutual attraction or will they once again deny what they feel.

**Taming the Wolff**—Del Robertson ONLY ONE WOMAN... As devastatingly beautiful as she is headstrong, noble-born Alexis DeVale abruptly finds her preordained life in upheaval. Abducted at sword-point, held for ransom, thrust into a maelstrom of lawlessness and piracy... HAS THE POWER... The strength of her passion, the depth of her love... TO TAME THE WOLFF... Mayhem. Brutality. Murder. These are the tools of the trade - and Kris Wolff is the master of her profession. Captain of the high seas, a roguish pirate, her heart hardened by life, her passion tightly controlled by the secret she's forced to keep. Faced with a new danger, The Wolff finds herself unable to guard her heart from the tumultuous desires that Alexis DeVale has awakened.

**Private Dancer**—TJ Vertigo Reece Corbett grew up on the mean streets on New York City, abused, used and in trouble with the law. Faith Ashford grew up wealthy, with all the creature comforts that money provides. When they meet fireworks begin.

**Miriam and Esther**—Sherry Barker Miriam thought her life would play out in the bustling metropolis of Dallas, but after a life-changing accident, she moves to the small town of Cool Lake, Texas to get her head on straight and regain her senses.

**McKee**—A.C. Henley Private Investigator Quinlan McKee has returned to Los Angeles after a three-year absence, only to find herself embroiled in a world of child slavery and police corruption.

E-Books, Print, Free e-books

Visit our website for more publications available online.

www.affinityebooks.com

Published by Affinity E-Book Press NZ LTD
Canterbury, New Zealand

Registered Company 2517228

Printed in Great Britain
by Amazon.co.uk, Ltd.,
Marston Gate.